Cry Down Dark

T.J. Tranchell

Blysster Press

Email the author at: tj@warning-signs.net
Website: www.warning-signs.net
Facebook: www.facebook.com/TJTranchell

"Cry Down Dark" Printing History
Blysster Press paperback edition March 2016

Blysster Press

A new kind of publisher for a new kind of world.

This is a work of fiction. Names, characters, places, and incidents either are the product of the author's imagination or are used fictitiously. Any resemblance to actual persons, living or dead, events, business establishments, or locales is entirely coincidental.

ISBN 978-1-940247-24-3

Printed in the United States of America
www.blysster.com

For JRS

who started this

and

Savannah

who finished it

THANK YOU

Cry Down Dark would not have been possible without a number of friends and family and it is impossible to name them all. With apologies to those not named, I'd like to thank: Leslie Tranchell, Deken Loveless, Logan Loveless, Mandy Cloward, Laurie Olson, Amy Tranchell, Stacie Tranchell and all significant others; Tom and Roze Tranchell, Sandi Greer-Gatlin, Steve Cummings and Sue Stevens, the Gibsons, Pam and Mark Weiss, and Billie Gold.

Professionally and academically, I owe thanks to: John Ziebell, Shawn O'Neal, Brandon Schrand, Liahna Armstrong, and Lisa Norris.

Huge thanks to those who read and edited this: Ryan Bailey and Chip Erekson.

To Charity Becker, who listened to me pitch books two years in row at Crypticon and didn't blink when I finally sent her a complete draft of the first one.

Nothing I've written would have ended up on the page without my mom, DeeAnna Erekson.

I wouldn't be writing this now without the love and support of my wife Savannah and our son Clark.

Finally, this book is for my grandma Vilda Erekson, who passed away hours after it was accepted for publication.

CHAPTER

~1~

The first time Peter Toombs saw Diana in her wedding dress was at the funeral. Her sisters dressed her the day before, he had heard, and she appeared as she had in the pictures. Mostly. The smile was there and a certain gleam to her skin. *But the light*, Peter thought, *the light is gone*.

He'd driven ten hours to get there—almost the entire drive on one lonely road—and made it just in time to get the last parking space at the funeral home. A snow flurry followed Peter through the door. Not everyone turned toward him when he entered the lobby, and most of those who did showed no signs of recognition. The faces that did recognize him froze Peter more than the blizzard that raged in the sky on his drive from Reno.

Except one. Diana's brother David waved and smiled at Peter from the viewing room. Peter maneuvered through the crowd, brushing snow off his coat and on to many of the other mourners. A few whispers—"I can't believe he showed up" and "What is he doing here"—reached his ears before he reached the casket. Once there, David pushed back a hovering group to allow Peter some space.

"Mom won't like this," David said, "but I know Diana would. Be sure to say hi to Debbie, though."

"Thank you; I will," Peter said, the hoarseness of

crying and ten hours of singing the same album in the car not yet clear from his voice. "You are the only one who knows how much this hurts me." Peter shook David's hand and then turned his focus to the woman in the coffin.

Peter could hear the whispering spreading through the funeral home but did his best to ignore it. He bent over the casket and kissed Diana on the cheek and lightly on the lips. Years had passed since Peter had kissed a woman with love on his mind and he wasn't sure he ever would again. He moved to take her hand and kiss it, also, but a heavier hand fell on his shoulder.

"You aren't the only one here to see her, Toombs."

"Just give me a few minutes, please." Peter turned slightly to see who had interrupted him. He recognized Aaron Doyle from the wedding photos he saw on his way in. Aaron and Diana had been married less than three years before Diana succumbed to the brain tumor. Peter's one chance at meeting Aaron had passed when Peter was not invited to the wedding.

"Your time is up. You're lucky I'm letting you stay." Aaron turned sharply and walked into Diana's parents. The three exchanged hugs and whispers before entering the chapel. Aaron glanced back at Peter once again, his teeth clenched against the desire to tear Peter's throat out.

You can't get to me, Peter thought, *not today. I've seen more poison from production assistants.*

Peter let the snow in again when he went out for air. One last breather before the ceremony to replace the one last cigarette he would have smoked last year. David followed him but stopped at the door.

"You're coming back, Peter, aren't you?" David called through the growing storm.

"Yes, David, just give me a moment." Peter didn't turn to see how long David lingered at the door. He hoped David wouldn't spend too much time worrying about him, alienating himself from his family. They hated Peter enough. He hoped that wouldn't spill over to David.

Peter walked to his car, not bothering to shake the snow from his bushy red hair. He gazed up into the sky and, taking advantage of the howling wind, decided to scream. *I'm not usually the one who screams*, he thought, while his mouth filled with snow and more flakes stuck to his goatee. *They all know it, too. They don't know what to think, just sitting there waiting for me to do something scary. Good thing none of them are seeing this.*

More people watched when he re-entered the funeral home. Maybe some of them heard the scream. Maybe the rumors have spread, like a virus. He could tell many of them were doing their best not to whisper. *More like madness*, he thought. He made his way to a seat in the back corner that David had reserved for him. He felt like he was parading for everyone who could see. Get a good look; this circus is a one night only show.

Peter sat down and zoned out for most of the service. After eulogies from Diana's father and a friend of Aaron's, the service director asked if anyone else would like to say anything. Many of the heads Peter had been staring at the backs of swiveled to return the favor. He'd not planned on saying anything but was loath to disappoint an audience. Especially one that wasn't going anywhere. He took his time walking to the podium giving more people a longer chance to stare. Come one and all! See the Geek eat live chickens!

When he arrived at the podium Peter turned to face the sea of mourners riding the waves of grief and anger. Many faces held the stare of frozen hatred he'd seen earlier, as frosty and uninviting as the storm outside. Some lit up like they were seeing him for the first time. Like they'd just realized he was somebody, not just the whisper they'd been hearing for the last hour and a half.

"My name is Peter Toombs." He heard a small gasp after saying his name. "I met Diana back when we were in high school. This was years before many of you met her. All of you know how special she is otherwise you wouldn't be here. Some of you know that our relationship ended poorly. All that is over. But I never stopped caring about her.

"Thank you, Aaron, for making her happy during your time together. I can't imagine you heard anything good about me but I only heard good of you.

"Thank you, David, for making me feel welcome. Do you think if any of these people knew who I was before now they'd have treated me differently? Perhaps.

"Thank you to those who made Diana so beautiful today. I'm glad I got to see her in her wedding dress.

"You may not believe it but I loved Diana. I still do. I can't change what happened between us and I can't bring her back. God knows I wish I could." Peter started crying, again, as did many of the attendees. He vacated the podium, walking before all those eyes again when a little girl popped out in front of him.

She wrapped her arms around his legs, peering up into his tear-filled eyes. Her large blue eyes reminded Peter too much of Diana's brown eyes.

"Don't worry, Mr. Toombs," she said. "She'll come back for you."

CHAPTER

~2~

Peter Toombs, at age twenty-four, was not used to being scared. He'd left that behind at age fifteen during a night in juvenile detention. Before that, the boogeyman and all the nightmares that came with him ran Peter's life. Now he was the boogeyman for millions of readers and moviegoers around the country. There were times of heightened anxiety and anticipation, of course. Like before the signing of his contract for *Graveyard Paradise*, his television show. Motivational anxiety, his philosophy professor had said, is good fear. Peter wasn't sure how motivational it was but fears had provided him with a good living. He wasn't Stephen King-rich or even Clive Barker-rich, but he was sure he made more money than everyone at Diana's funeral. Hell, he probably made more than all of them combined.

His last novel, *Takes My Life*, had been nominated for the Stoker Award and long-listed for the National Book Award, among others. The rarity of this praise for a horror novel—not to mention that it was only Peter's second published novel—was accompanied by a tidal wave of uproar and publicity. Peter was in a hotel in Seattle when he learned Diana was back in the hospital; Peter was home in Reno when the news of her death reached him. Not until after the funeral did Peter remember that he could be scared, too.

CHAPTER

~3~

The little girl, the one who hugged him, her name was Esmeralda. She was Diana's niece from her older sister Dawn and only three years old on the day of the funeral. Aaron and Diana didn't have children of their own so Essie was the next best thing.

Essie, the blue-eyed girl who reminded Peter so much of brown-eyed Diana, put fear back in Peter's heart. *Don't worry, Mr. Toombs*, he heard her say. *She'll come back for you.*

She'll come back for you.

Back for you.

For you.

You.

During the graveside service, Peter kept telling himself that Essie caught his name from the impromptu eulogy or maybe from one of the other mourners. She couldn't have known who he was. That part he could explain. He could always explain. That's what he did; explain all the weird shit that happens to people every day.

So why was she smiling?

In a room full of grief, one little girl found a smile for the most hated man in the building. Every day that smile scared Peter a little further out of his mind.

There was more to it than just that. The eyes, the

smile, the way she'd walked right up to Peter, all reminded him of someone he should have known. A person linking Diana and Peter together. He blocked out the thoughts that nearly surfaced, knowing they would come back to him at some other time. While many of the good ideas got away, most of the bad ones did not.

He moved out of Reno and into a home less than three miles from Diana's grave. Waiting for the right house took four months. Purchasing it under his agent's name took another two months. Although he knew someone was bound to see him, he wanted to avoid anyone knowing he was coming to town until he was there in the flesh.

Peter drove the same desolate highway he traveled half a year earlier, in the heat of summer this time instead of the snows of winter. Even without the blizzard he had trouble seeing. While the CD playing during his last trip was safely packed away, the memories were not. Through the tears, Peter managed to sing most of the songs without the album.

The sun hadn't set when Peter crossed the town line into Bern, the imitation Swiss village high in the Wasatch Mountains of Utah. There was just enough time to stop by the cemetery before dusk, before the gates closed for the night. Instead, Peter stopped at the town diner and had a cheeseburger. Peter, for all he knew, went unnoticed.

***

Diana and her family had moved out of Bern just after her freshman year in high school. While many of their friends remained, much of the extended family moved on as well. That was how Peter came to purchase Diana's childhood home.

He could see it from the sidewalk outside the diner and Peter knew he'd be able to see it from the cemetery.

David pointed it out to him during the graveside service. The three-bedroom house sat on a small hill on the eastern edge of town. From the front porch, you could see most of Bern, according to the real estate agent Peter dealt with. From the back, you could see the mountains and not much else.

The Wards had left the home when the family reached six children, David and Diana being the fourth and fifth, respectively, and Debbie the youngest. While their time in Bern would only be a few more years, it was a place stamped on Diana's heart. She specifically asked to be buried there. She'd told Peter about Bern often over French fries during high school and later over beers during their first years of college. They'd talked about settling here, having children, growing old.

Peter had grown up in a small town called Blackhawk, less than forty miles from Bern, but he didn't hold the same attachment to his town as Diana held for Bern. For Peter any small town would do. They never argued about it; it would be small town living for them. But when Peter left college for New York and then Hollywood, he gave up the idea of ever seeing Bern.

I'm here now, he thought. Tonight, he would be sleeping in Diana's house, now his house. He tried guessing which room she had slept in, thinking maybe he'd sleep there.

A train whistle blew and a flock of birds took off into the sky, following their own lonely highways. Watching the small birds leave, Peter wished for them to come back.

She'll come back for you.

The statement, clear as the train whistle, came back to him. From the forest behind his new house, he could hear owls screeching, crying down the dark. Trying to speed up the sunset so they could hunt. Any noise is good noise; it is the silence that can get to you.

Peter drove the short distance from the diner to the house without taking his eyes off the front porch. No other cars were on the road. The families of Bern already settled for the evening, some just finishing supper, some in the midst of prime-time television. Many of the houses had mini-satellite dishes, ruining the effect of the Swiss village. There was a good chance that someone in Bern had seen *Graveyard Paradise*, the cable TV show that he had created and written for its first season. If the show had turned out how he wanted it, everyone would have seen his face. Diana was the only person he'd told, but most of his other friends knew he wanted to be Rod Serling.

You are about to enter a world not of sight or sound, but of mind. Welcome ... to *The Twilight Zone*. Peter whistled the theme music as he walked up the steps to his front door. He was in the Zone, all right. That funeral was an episode waiting to happen.

Essie would have fit perfectly in one of those early *Twilight Zone* shows. *Graveyard Paradise* had more in common with *Tales from the Crypt* than *Twilight Zone*. Any cute little girl on Peter's show usually ended up in little pieces, not giggling and being creepy.

Peter felt right at home as he crossed the threshold. The movers put everything in the same order they packed it up from his house in Reno. Not everything would be in the same place, he knew, but having that instant sense of home helped alleviate some of the tension he'd expected. He walked through the front room into the kitchen, pleased that he wouldn't have to move around any furniture. The refrigerator had been stocked up by the real estate agent. All the things he needed were here. There was a 12-pack of Smirnoff Ice, a drink he disdained until finding out it had become Diana's favorite alcoholic beverage.

Peter and Diana used to drink Heineken together, trying to feel superior to the Bud and Miller Lite drinkers they knew. Now Peter was hooked on this flat, Kool-Aid tasting thing that floated in the bottle like dirty water.

He twisted the cap off a bottle and chugged down a third of its contents, mixing it up with the greaseburger he'd just eaten. At least the drink was cold. Like the air blowing through the house.

He'd forgotten to shut the door, that small-town mentality coming back sooner than he thought. He knew why. When he came to live here, he thought he'd be carrying Diana across the threshold. He was still carrying her, though, like an anchor holding down his heart. *Perhaps when she comes back*, he thought, *I can carry her for real.*

CHAPTER

~4~

Diana didn't come back that first night. Peter went to the Bern cemetery after breakfast the next day. He walked around, cataloguing some of the headstones, getting himself together for the inevitable flood that would soon be upon him.

The oldest markers were from the wagon train days, early Mormon settlers than never made it to Salt Lake City. The newest was Diana's. Bern had strict regulations on who could be buried in their cemetery. The cemetery hadn't played host to a graveside service in the five years previous to Diana's mid-winter internment. The groundskeepers were paid well and earned their keep. Sprinklers watered the southwest quadrant as Peter made his way to the plot on the slope of the northwest corner.

The grass marking her plot struggled to take root and Peter could understand the grass's hesitance to accept the fact of its newest charge. The headstone, a piece of petrified wood half the size of a Volkswagen, seemed to be more in its place than the patch of sparse grass. A picture of Diana, one of her wedding photos in profile, had been etched into the face of the marker, next to her name and dates. The epitaph "Daughter, Sister, Wife, Friend" let everyone know who paid for the rock.

A sentiment like that must have angered Aaron, her husband. The clenched jaw of Diana's widower flashed through Peter's memory. Just because she was their kid first didn't mean he, Aaron, had loved her any less. Peter had been telling himself something similar for years: just because he wasn't with her didn't mean he loved her any less.

"Hi, Diana," Peter said to the picture on the marker. "Here we both are, your hometown. Just like we always talked about. I even bought your old house. It's a bit drafty, but I don't mind. I've only been here one night, but I feel at home. Funny how things turn out.

"Anyway. I'll come see you often. I figured if I'm here you won't have as far to come get me."

The southwest sprinklers shut off and the northwest sprinklers came on. Peter didn't notice until a jet of water hit him in the ear.

CHAPTER

~5~

Peter spent the rest of the day walking around Bern. All the buildings along Main Street had snow-white trim and many were painted a sky-blue color rarely seen outside of The Sound of Music. From one doorway—an insurance agency of all places— Peter could hear a music box version of "Edelweiss." He heard it again from a hair salon on the next block.

Despite being the middle of summer, Peter found himself in the mood for a cup of hot chocolate. Maybe one with those little marshmallows floating near the top. Wait until winter and there would be more hot chocolate than Peter could handle.

The thought of winter and the accompanying storms caused Peter to briefly shiver and to remind him of his last visit to this town. Before he could start another sobbing spell, he noticed a sign reading "Bern Bookseller." He hesitated before entering, knowing that if he was to be recognized, it would likely be here.

Fuck it, he thought. It wouldn't kill him to shake a few hands, maybe sign a few books. Might do the place some good.

He'd helped a few local bookstores in Reno increase their trade. Peter made it a point not to sign in major chain stores, knowing they'd sell his books anyway. He preferred the small establishments, sometimes even appearing at comic book stores. After the release of the first season of *Graveyard Paradise* on DVD, the comic shops became one of his biggest draws. He'd even signed a few T-shirts.

A cuckoo clock inside the Bern Bookseller hit the hour just after Peter closed the door. He noticed the bird inside the clock was a raven. That feeling of coming home increased just a little.

"Admiring our cuckoo, sir?" a voice said from around the corner of a shelf. The voice belonged to a small, elderly man holding a feather duster.

"Yes, I am. Just my style," Peter replied with a smile for the man who was no doubt the proprietor.

"Not surprised. A fellow like you, that clock would be right up your alley." The man winked at Peter's surprised face. Peter was not expecting to be recognized quite that soon.

"You're right there. Pleased to meet you." Peter held his hand out. The man switched the feather duster to his left hand and grasped Peter's offered hand. The grip was firm and Peter began to doubt his original perception of the man's age.

"Pleased as well, Mr. Toombs. We don't get too many best-selling authors in here." The man winked again, still holding Peter's hand. "I'm Ben Hill. Don't laugh; that's my name."

Peter momentarily saw this slight man running around like a fool, being chased by bikini-clad buxom beauties. The image didn't quite seem to fit but Peter almost did laugh.

"You're laughing, Mr. Toombs. From your work one would think you never laughed."

"Please, call me Peter and I promise not to call you Benny."

"Deal," Ben said, pumping Peter's hand one last time before relinquishing it.

"So," Ben continued, "what brings you to the Bern

Bookseller? If you are trying to find our writers' reference section, I'd say you are doing fine and should select something else."

"No, I just moved in and I'm checking out the town. I bought one of the old houses up on the hill."

"Ah, yes. The old Ward home. Poor girl. I don't expect you heard about her, being just new in town."

Peter didn't know if he should say he did know or if he should let Ben tell him the story. Ben didn't give him time to choose. "First burial we had in five years. Young lady, Diana Ward—I guess her stone would say Diana Doyle, seeing as how she'd married—caught a brain tumor and passed before she reached 24. I missed the service myself but I heard this old boyfriend—" Ben stopped and looked right into Peter's eyes. "You do know. That was you. What did that little girl say to you? They say you turned whiter than the snow. No one yet has seen fit to tell me what she said."

"She said, 'Don't worry, Mr. Toombs. She'll come back for you.'"

"Really now?" Ben didn't sound surprised at all. "Knowing her as a child, Diana that is, I just bet she will, too."

CHAPTER

~6~

Peter stood there, mouth agape, for long enough to worry Ben.

"Mr. Toombs? Peter?" Ben said, reaching out to him. "Are you still with us?"

"Still here," Peter finally said, shaking the static from his brain. "What did you mean just then?"

"Well, you know," Ben's voice took a nervous tone before once again becoming the jolly tenor Peter had first heard. "It's just that Diana was a girl so full of love that I always thought she'd do anything for someone she cared for. Why, I remember when she was five. Her cat, Jelly-Bean she called it, died. Little Diana spent three days sitting by the backyard grave her daddy dug, waiting for the cat to come back."

"Three days," Peter repeated, trying to remember if Diana ever spoke about her cat. "Just like Jesus."

"That's it exactly. Diana said the same thing. Of course, the cat never returned, but I'm sure Diana never doubted that it would. She simply altered her expected timeline for feline resurrection."

Peter was firmly back in *The Twilight Zone*, which wasn't surprising. Now that he thought of it, Peter noticed just how much Ben Hill, proprietor, looked like Burgess

Meredith.

"Anyway," Ben said, now moving back to his shelves. "I wouldn't spend too much time concerning yourself with such thoughts. There's time enough now for other matters."

Yes. Time enough now. Just like old Burgess said in that episode where all he wanted was time to read. Don't worry, Mr. Toombs, you're only waist deep in weirdness. Just wait until it gets to your neck. Peter hoped this would be as far as the weirdness went. He hadn't been this deep in it since…

Since he and Diana had split up.

"Peter? Would you mind signing this copy of *Takes My Life*? It's the only one we have in stock, I'm afraid. Guess I'll need to order more if you'll be around for a while."

CHAPTER

~7~

Peter should have felt hungry for lunch by the time he left the Bern Bookseller and Ben Hill to continue his dusting within. The thought of food after spending time with Ben Hill didn't feel right. Maybe he'd just have a milkshake and perhaps some onion rings.

Apparently Ben had gone to the phone instead of back to his dusting. Ten people looked up as Peter took a corner booth in the diner. The night before, despite a somewhat larger crowd, no one had looked at him. He'd even had difficulty getting the waitress to notice him. Now, six women and four men fixed him with stares slightly more than curious. Peter decided he'd have his order to go.

Before the waitress could get to him, one of the women took it upon her to greet him. She slid into the booth next to Peter. Not the other side that would have been too formal. She made one of those farting noises as she slid on the vinyl-covered bench but both she and Peter ignored it. Although Peter had tried to stop guessing ages just on appearance, if he had to say, this one was in her mid-thirties. No more than thirty-five. Her sleeveless blue sundress hugged the curves of her body, revealing a scene no less spectacular than the Swiss Alps her ancestors had hiked out of. Peter wondered how often she put her hair in long ponytails. He chuckled, a thing he hated others doing. At that moment, he gladly would have bet anyone her name was Heidi.

"Hi," she said, thrusting her bosom against Peter's arm. "I'm Helga. You just moved in, didn't you?" He would have lost money on that one, but you had to give him credit for being close.

"Yes, I did. How about you?"

"Nope. Lived in Bern my whole life. Have I seen you before?"

"Depends. You might try asking Mr. Hill at the bookstore."

"Oh, he already called here. He didn't say you were so attractive." That made Peter laugh again. A distinct lack of attractiveness, the uncontrollable red hair sprouting from the top of his head, kept him from being the face of the show he created.

"Helga," a stronger female voice bellowed from the kitchen. "Get back to your salad and leave the nice man alone."

"Sorry, Penny," Helga said. She went back to her stool at the counter. Before sitting, she turned and blew a kiss at Peter. He made no move to catch it. Helga returned to her Chicken Caesar.

Peter recalled the other woman as being the waitress who "served" him the previous night. *She must own the place to be here so much*, he thought.

"What'll you have, sugar?" Penny asked him. "Cheeseburger again?" She had a better memory than Peter's; he'd thought her name to be Laura last night. Penny, embossed on her nametag above "Wilkommen to der Bern Diner" suited her just right.

"Not today, thanks," Peter said, sounding more cheerful than he felt. "Just a milkshake and an order of onion rings."

"Choc, van, or straw?"

"Chocolate, please."

"Want that malted?" Peter hadn't had a malted since high school. The one remaining malt shop in Blackhawk closed just before he graduated.

"Absolutely," he answered.

"OK. One chocolate malted and a dish of rings. Anything else?"

"Nope, that should do it. Don't spare on the whipped cream or the ranch and I'll be a happy camper." He was starting to feel it, too. He'd forgotten about getting his order to go. Penny put her order pad in the pocket of her apron and went back behind the counter. She began preparing his malt just after hanging his order on the roundabout.

Peter was sure they used real ice cream here, too. Bern, even with Helga and Ben Hill to creep him out, might be heaven after all.

Penny timed it perfectly and Peter's malt arrived with his onion rings. He could sense how perfect the contrast between the fried onion rings and the cold malt would be. Even Helga gossiping and occasionally peeking over her shoulder at him couldn't ruin it.

He managed to eat three onion rings, covered in ranch dressing, before the next interruption. His new visitor had the courtesy to sit across from him instead of next to him. The man was the only person wearing a suit that Peter had seen since leaving Reno. He sat with both palms flat on the table, looking straight ahead at Peter.

"May I help you?" Peter asked.

"Yes, Mr. Toombs, I believe you may." His cuff links and law school lapel pin announced the man's professionalism. He looked like he'd be more comfortable in an office in Denver or Tacoma. Not New York, though. Not yet.

"Would you care for an onion ring?" Peter held out a

bread-battered circle to the stranger. Eating the few rings he'd had so far had awakened the hunger he previously denied. Peter truly hoped the man would refuse the proffered delicacy.

"No, thank you, Mr. Toombs. I've not been able yet to purchase a plot in our cemetery. I've no plans to perish from a grease-induced heart attack."

"Stress-induced, then? Who are you?"

"Forgive me." The man's right hand went into his suit coat and pulled out a business card. "Walter Lerner, attorney-at-law and Bern city councilman."

"Bern is large enough to have a city council?" Peter asked. He put the onion ring he held into the dish of dressing then into his mouth.

"Barely. We take turns serving among those desiring and deserving to serve. Stay here long enough and you may well have an opportunity to serve."

"To paraphrase something I heard recently, I've no intention to perish from a conscience-induced heart attack. What do you want, Mr. Lerner?"

"Merely to say hello and offer a welcome."

"You were beat to the punch by Helga over there, not to mention Mr. Hill at the bookstore."

"Ah, yes. Two of Bern's wonderful characters. I assume that is why you are here. To meet new characters?"

"You assume incorrectly."

"Then why are you here?"

"To live in a quiet place while one still exists."

"You've no alterior motives for Bern? Or its cemetery?"

And there it was. This hick lawyer in his banker's suit wanted to keep Peter out of the cemetery.

"First of all, you mean *ulterior* motives. And if I did have any other reasons for being here, I wouldn't tell a junior gangster like you. So, if you don't have anything else to say,

I'd like to finish my malt and onion rings in peace. Alone."

Lerner stood up, the color rising in his cheeks as he did so. "Stay out of the cemetery, Toombs. Or we will have to keep you out."

Peter took a long pull from the straw in his malt. He dipped and ate another ring, all while Lerner stood there looking insulted. Peter ate two more rings before Lerner finally left.

Maybe I should have let Helga stay, Peter thought. *She was much better company.*

CHAPTER
~8~

No one bothered Peter at the diner again. He would stop in every other day or so. During his first week in Bern, Peter made it a point not to go to the cemetery. To let Lerner think he'd intimidated Peter into staying away. That didn't stop him from walking or driving by the gates at least once a day. Every time he did there was always another car or another walker right there.

If this was how they'd planned to keep Peter out, they would have to try harder. He would slow down just enough for whoever was watching to get nervous. If he was walking, he'd stop at the gate and peer inside. Once he heard the footsteps behind him get too close, he'd started walking again. Sometimes he looked back. Mostly, Peter pretended not to know he was being watched.

Peter had to make a game of it. It was the only way he could deal with the situation and not get upset. Or worse, not get royally pissed off.

After two weeks of this, this sentry-like presence, Peter let the person watching him catch up. Peter made a hard turn into the graveyard and ran until he reached its center. Like Captain Kidd or Robert Johnson, he thought. My fate will be decided at a crossroads.

He turned to face this citizen of Bern, the one who

drew today's watch. He was a man Peter recognized from the diner and from at least two other days of this routine.

"Mr. Toombs," he said. "You aren't supposed to be in here." He wasn't quite panting but, from his breathing, Peter could tell he wasn't ready for such a quick jog.

"Do you know why I'm not allowed in the cemetery?" Peter asked. Sweat began rolling down Peter's forehead, pushing him toward a boiling point.

"Councilman Lerner told us to keep you out, that's all I know. And if he or the constable finds out you got in here, my ass will be spending the night in the cell."

Peter laughed at the words the cell, a clear image of Bern's one-room jail popping into his head. He could see the constable twirling a ring of keys on one finger, his cowboy-booted feet propped up on the desk.

"Don't laugh, Mr. Toombs. They'll lock me up for sure."

"If they are this serious about keeping me out, I don't doubt that they will. Of course, they'd have to find out I made it in. How will they know if you don't tell?"

"Mr. Toombs, do you really think that I'm the only one watching right now?"

CHAPTER
~9~

Josh Sebold, Peter's sentry for the day, told Peter all about the town meeting Lerner held the day after meeting Peter. About how not everyone showed up but they all got the message anyway. They were to be as nice to Peter as they could, really make him feel at home, but only when they saw him around town. Which would explain why everyone he saw smiled and waved and called him by name. They must have my picture circulating the area, he thought.

It also explained why no one yet had come up to the house to chat or ask for a signed book. Although he'd only had one book out at the time and was commuting to L.A. twice a month to work on the TV show, a certain section of the population knew who he was when he'd moved into his first apartment there. Before Peter did any signings, two dozen people had shown up at his door with copies of that first book, *Scream Queen*, hoping to get close to someone who was getting close to fame. They were like a little club; young adults all dressed in black, black eyeliner and nail polish. The ones that had to take all the metal out of their faces when they went to their jobs at Burger King or the grocery store. He knew these kids; he'd been one himself.

He'd seen a few of them around Bern, too. He could see them straining with desire to approach him, to talk with him. Instead, they'd wave like everyone else and keep on walking. He noticed one of them with the *Graveyard Paradise* comic book adaptations and hoped for a chance to sign for a real fan. The kid practically ran from Peter, like he'd catch leprosy if he talked to Peter.

The older residents of Bern weren't so shy. They'd approach him on the street with copies of *Takes My Life* (always the new one, never *Scream Queen*. Like the list of awards and nominations made it OK to read or at least have on one's shelf) and ask how things were going, if he was working on anything new. They'd shake his hand, say thank you and be on their way. Peter watched a few of them walk away from him and could see the fake joviality shrug off their shoulders the moment he was out of hearing range.

All this he thought of while Sebold continued his confession. None of them were to mention anything to Peter about the cemetery or the Ward family. If Peter asked about either of these topics, they were to refer him to Councilman Lerner. And no one, not even the one pizza delivery guy, was to visit Peter at home. The eyes were everywhere. Maybe after a while, things would calm down, Sebold implied, but for now the town's hackles were up.

Peter wanted to ask more questions but knew he wouldn't get anything more out of Josh Sebold today. He was, in fact, lucky to garner the bits of information he'd been supplied with. As they reached the cemetery gates, Peter thanked Sebold and told him to call if he needed anything or got in trouble.

"You're welcome," Sebold said. "Don't think me rude but I likely won't make that call. I got family here and always have. I'd like to keep it that way." He watched, his appointed task, as Peter turned back toward home instead of town like he'd been headed before their interlude. About ten minutes later, Walter Lerner arrived to relieve Sebold of his duties.

CHAPTER
~10~

Peter sat in his living room. The living room of a dead woman he loved. Just because she hadn't lived in the house for the majority of the last decade did not bother Peter. He sat watching his own copy of *Graveyard Paradise* Season One. He enjoyed watching the show despite the multitude of creative differences he had experienced while working on it. Like not seeing his own face every show. His friend Connor Parrish held that honor and still did well into *Graveyard Paradise*'s third season. Peter couldn't blame Connor; hell, Peter got him the job once it was determined that the host job would not be Peter's.

At the time, Connor wasn't much more than a working actor, specializing in the better class of slasher films. Peter met him at a horror convention and the two hit it off superbly. Now, Connor was still in Hollywood, killing starlets on-screen and boinking them off-screen. Peter had retreated, first back to Reno and then to Bern.

Where he sat, digesting the information that an entire town had conspired to keep him isolated and away from the one thing he came to this town to do. In the cemetery, he'd planned on talking to Diana, or at least to the picture carved into her headstone. There no pictures of her in the house; Peter didn't have any worth hanging. He had a box full

35

of snapshots and one small portrait taken of her just before graduating from Blackhawk High that he kept in his wallet. He had home videos of her that he'd taped himself at various events but that was too much. Every time he watched one of those tapes he wanted to slit his wrists. Even before she died, he felt that way. Watching the happy moments before the break-up was like watching a ghost he could rewind, fast-forward, or pause. The specter of those tapes was like a poltergeist that follows a person even when they leave the house where it began. He knew where they were if he wanted them.

Then, there was always the cassette. Peter put that thought out of his mind as soon as he had it. Things weren't that bad.

What would Diana think of her idyllic little town treating him like a pariah? Her parents and Aaron would probably think it was just fine. That Peter was finally getting what he deserved after all this time. But Diana? Her body was stuck here forever. If she knew what was going on, would she still want to be associated with this place? Or was she rolling in her grave right now, trying to get out so she can leave, coming back for Peter on her way out of town?

She'd been happy here, Peter knew. Happier than all the time she had spent with him and perhaps happier than all the time after. She wanted to come back here at the end. She spent her honeymoon at the bed and breakfast overlooking Bern from a hill opposite the one her house stood on. There was a reason she wanted to be here. Peter would find out why.

And he would discover why the townsfolk went along with Walter Lerner's determination that Peter be kept out of the cemetery. He'd learn, by crook or by hook, why he was really here. And just what that little girl meant.

"I'm here, Diana," Peter said to the air and anything else that might be listening. "Tell me what to do."

CHAPTER
~11~

A longtime student of horror film and fiction, Peter expected to have at least one portentous dream and more than his share of nightmares. Alas, no dreams other than his usual had occurred. He suffered nightly through his common dream-stew of sex with famous women (some he even knew and one he dated) and his own mythology that inspired many of his better short stories. While many of the faces were familiar, the situations never were. And none of the faces were Diana's.

In all his life, he only knew of one recurring dream and he'd not had this dream since that night in detention. In the dream, a giant is chasing him. No matter how close the giant is or how far away, Peter can hear its footsteps. Sometimes, the giant has a normal pace, just reminding Peter that he is still right behind him. Other times the giant's footsteps come much faster and much louder, the giant trying to run Peter down. Never once did the giant ever catch up, never so much as touched Peter. As a child, he was absolutely positive there was a giant after him and that one night it would catch him and he wouldn't wake up. If he was nervous, the giant ran faster and louder. As a teen, and after finally understanding what Edgar Allan Poe was talking about, Peter realized that the footsteps of the giant were the beats of his own heart. His heart kept beating after that, but the giant no longer chased him.

How many people knew about the giant in his head and in his chest? Peter could only think of one person he'd ever told. Not his mom or his sister, no. Only Diana. She knew. What was it she told him?

You have the heart of a giant, so full of love that it must scare you. It scares me, too.

Don't be afraid, he had answered. I'd never do anything to hurt you.

Don't make promises you aren't sure you can keep, Diana said. Like she knew what was coming.

CHAPTER

~12~

He woke up, still in his chair, staring at 37 inches of Connor Parrish's face and *Graveyard Paradise* logo. That was the beauty of DVDs: no rewinding required. Once the disc was done, it went right back to the menu. Connor grinned at him, showing too many teeth. The casting director did not believe Peter when he told her about that grin. The only other work she could find of Connor's had him behind a mask or thick make-up. With this gig, Connor finally got to be himself. Or, as Peter tried not to think of too often, he got to be Peter Toombs. Peter wanted to believe there were no hard feelings, but that wasn't true. He only had to listen to his commentary track, done by himself, not even a P.A. in the room to know that.

He clicked off the TV and thought about spending the rest of the night in the chair. In the right position, it was just as comfortable as the bed he slept on. He stood up and walked down the hall and up the stairs. If he turned left, he would go into the master bedroom. If he turned right, he would head toward the bathroom and another bedroom. He turned right and passed the bathroom door, reaching in to turn off the light as he went.

He stood in front of the open bedroom door, still hesitant after a week of sleeping in this room. He'd tried the bedroom downstairs first but it was too hot. That and he didn't feel Diana in the room. Peter had been telling himself that he would be able to feel which room Diana had spent her childhood in. The truth was he didn't really feel her in this room, either. She'd never said anything about sleeping in the master bedroom post-cradle and there were only the two other bedrooms.

The one he peered into now had most recently been the room of a baseball-loving boy, according to the wallpaper. Bats, balls and mitts were scattered along three walls with the fourth painted to look like a crowd-filled stadium. Even the carpet was green and not completely unlike Astroturf. The closet, currently containing a few jackets Peter had hung there, was built to resemble a clubhouse locker.

While he didn't feel Diana in the room, Peter was reminded of his and Diana's scare during her senior year. He would have been seven and (hopefully) in love with baseball much as Peter had been around that age. Peter hadn't thought of the baby that almost was—Kurt Vincent Toombs, his name would have been, after Kurt Cobain and Vincent Price —until he first stepped in the room. When was the last time he'd thought of Kurt? Peter couldn't remember.

Right now, in his moment of reflection, he thought again of Essie. How her blue eyes made him think of Diana's brown eyes. How maybe Kurt would have looked something like that: Diana's olive skin and round face with Peter's own blue eyes set there.

It was no one's fault that Diana had lost the baby. They both had wanted to keep it and her parents seemed OK with the decision. After the miscarriage, they'd stayed together almost two years. Perhaps the seeds of the hatred he felt from the Wards had begun there. He certainly harbored his own anger concerning the matter. But he never directed that hate upon Diana. Never intentionally, he reminded himself.

He crossed the turf to the small bed he kept there and laid down without undressing or pulling back the top sheet. While the owls screamed outside beneath the moonlight, Peter Toombs drifted to sleep and dreamt of going to see the Dodgers with his unborn son.

***

They bought Dodger Dogs even though Peter hated hotdogs. At one point, the TV cameras fell on them, projecting their image on the big screen. Peter was somebody and Kurt was somebody's kid. There had to be at least one movie star in attendance but they put Kurt and Peter up for everyone to see. Even the players on the field turned to look and cheer. Those players, though, weren't the current bunch of Boys in Blue. It was the 1988 team, from when Peter was eight years old, on the field. Peter had cheered hard for them that year in the World Series. There was catcher Mike Scioscia waving at him and Steve Sax and Mike Marshall smiling at Kurt. And "The Bulldog" Orel Hershiser, his glove hand resting against his thigh, nodded at both of them.

"No one is going to score on 55 today, are they, Daddy?" Kurt asked him.

"No, son, not today and not for the rest of the season. I promise." Peter tousled Kurt's hair then placed a blue cap on his head.

"Don't make a promise you can't keep, Daddy," Kurt said, nearly crying. Just then a foul ball came toward them. Neither got a glove on it and the ball hit Kurt in the head. He screamed, putting his face into Peter's stomach.

"Look, Daddy," Kurt bellowed. "I'm hurt and I'm bleeding Dodger Blue!" It was true; the front of Peter's road gray jersey was covered in a viscous blue substance. It didn't feel like blood, but it poured out of a deep cut on Kurt's head, spewing through the brand new ball cap Peter had put there moments before.

Peter looked out to the field in confusion. All the players were bleeding the same gooey blue substance. Even manager Tommy Lasorda had come onto the field, jets of blue spurting from his eyes. Peter's heart began to race. When he started to think that maybe he would have a heart attack he noticed who the visiting team was for this game.

As his heart raced faster and louder, Peter saw the uniforms of the San Francisco Giants.

CHAPTER
~13~

Most people at Diana's funeral didn't know much about her relationship with Peter. She might have told Aaron about the baby but Peter couldn't be sure. Most of her friends didn't know. Between the time she found out and the miscarriage happened, summer vacation had gotten well under way. It had been an interesting year anyway, what with Peter making monthly trips from college in Reno and Diana deciding if and where she would attend university. While her parents wanted her to stay close, with schools in Cedar City and Salt Lake City leading the pack, Peter did his best to convince her to come to Reno. After the miscarriage, she chose Reno. Before that, who knows? They could have been married or they could have split up then. It was rough going for a while. Diana eventually settled on Reno but only if Peter would take a semester off to stay with her in Blackhawk and get her ready for the move. She'd never been away from her parents; Peter was used to moving around with his mom. A semester off, after the hellish late spring and summer was a good idea, he agreed.

Diana's parents didn't think it such a good idea for her to spend so much time with Peter and especially didn't want her going to another state with a young man who'd impregnated her without them being married. In their Utah way, they still thought it a mortal sin to have sex out of wedlock.

Neither Peter nor Diana ever mentioned that they'd only done it once. Neither wanted to admit to being a cliché. The young man comes back from being away at college to take his high school sweetheart, a soon-to-graduate senior, to her senior prom. They end the night giving up their virginity to each other, not quite sure what they just did or if they did it right. He goes back to English 102 and she goes back to Home Economics. When her time of the month comes, it doesn't come. Once she is sure, she tells him. After finals are done he rushes to her side. They live happily ever after following the shotgun wedding and before the divorce.

OK, the last part doesn't happen. They don't get married and the baby never comes. Instead, on a record hot day in late June, Diana screams in pain and Peter rushed her to the hospital. The doctor comes out, covered in a bluish-red gunk (Look Daddy, I bleed Dodger Blue!) and says that Diana will be fine but they'll keep her for a few days' observation. The baby didn't make it. Later, the doctor takes him aside and asks if he wants to know whether it was a boy or a girl. Yes, he answers. It was a boy.

Little Kurt Vincent Toombs. The surprise that no one was ready for. Gone before he could begin. Not even far enough along to bother with a funeral. And despite all that, Peter and Diana stayed together. He never blamed her and she never blamed him. That doesn't mean Peter did not assign blame, oh no. He blamed God and made sure He knew it every chance he got.

So, yeah, there was a lot no one else knew. Peter liked it that way. He would have something with Diana that no other person on Earth could ever have. He had an almost son. He had an almost wife, which he hated to admit he did get one upped on. But that was life: someone always did better, had more, lived richer.

He also had something else that only David, Diana's brother, knew. He had a ring that he bought with his very first royalty check. Although he'd not seen Diana in two years, he meant to ask her to marry him. He was lucky to have run into David that day. He asked for directions to where Diana was staying. Instead David told him that Diana was engaged.

To be fair, Peter never should have come back. Diana had transferred to a different university after breaking up with Peter. There was nothing else in Blackhawk for him but the memory of Diana and the time they had together. With the sale of *Scream Queen* he thought Diana would forgive him and come running into his arms, ready to be his forever. More than just moving away from him, Diana had moved on with her life. She found someone to marry, someone to love. What had Peter done? He wrote and published a book he dedicated to her without her knowledge; he signed a huge contract for another book and a TV series; he dated women, rarely sleeping with any of them and never being part of anything with lasting potential. Yes, he had been very unfair.

But did he blame her? No. Did he blame himself? No. He blamed Diana's family (except David) and he blamed God. As happy as he wanted to be for her, going so far as to give David his address in hopes of receiving a wedding invitation, he just still held out hope of someday reuniting with her. He didn't think it would take a brain tumor for any progress to be made. Fuck you, God.

CHAPTER

~14~

The following morning, Peter received two phone calls. The first was from his agent, Leslie Laing. One of the producers of *Graveyard Paradise* wanted to meet with Peter and discuss a possible return to writing for them. Also, as every literary agent wants to know, Leslie asked if he was working on anything new. He told her he was—which wasn't a lie—and that it was pretty good—which was a lie. He'd not read through anything he'd written since coming to Bern but he knew shit when he wrote it. Leslie was satisfied and, after ascertaining that Peter would contemplate a return to the necromantic oasis he created, hung up.

Not even ten minutes later, the phone rang for the second time. It was Ben Hill of the Bern Bookseller. "Hi, Peter, how are you settling in?" he asked, seemingly unaware of the happenings between Peter and the townspeople.

"It is a small town, Mr. Hill, I'm surprised that you don't know by now," Peter answered, trying to keep his tone civil for such an early hour of the morning.

"Yes, yes. I've heard of your troubles. I was hoping you'd stop into the store so we could discuss it. And please, call me Ben."

"OK, Ben," Peter said, purposefully not hiding the suspicion in his voice. "What will we discuss?"

"What else? How to get you back with Diana. Come in around 8:30." Ben hung up before Peter could remind him that Ben's own store closed at 5 PM. Glancing at his watch, Peter made sure Ben did mean 8:30 at night. It was barely 9 AM and nearly time for his daily walk. Maybe Josh Sebold would be on duty today, he thought. Sebold hadn't been around since the day he ran into the cemetery.

While that didn't strike Peter as odd at the time, he made a mental note of it to ask Ben that evening. That is, unless he saw Sebold himself. If he did, he wouldn't need to ask Ben about him.

Peter didn't notice Josh Sebold near the cemetery and he wasn't at the diner when Peter popped in for lunch. He asked Penny but she stayed silent. He heard a muttering from the counter and attempted to pick out the speaker.

He couldn't, so he stopped thinking about it for the time being. People left small towns all the time. Peter himself had bailed out of three small towns rather unexpectedly during his short life. It happened all the time.

"It doesn't happen all the time. Not here."

Peter raised his eyes to see who had spoken. He took his cheeseburger out of his mouth without completing the bite he was about to take. He did not have to wait for the speaker to appear. Next to his table, Peter saw the bottom edge of a fraying sport coat. He looked further up where a law school pin just like the one he'd noticed in Walter Lerner's lapel gleamed from another suit. He craned further up still and discovered what Walter Lerner would look like in twenty years.

"People from Bern don't just up and leave. Least not as often as you'd think they would. No, either people move on and tell where they are going or they just disappear. You may argue that up and leaving without telling and disappearing are the same thing and I will have to differ with you on that, Mr. Toombs." Never once did the man Walter Lerner would become break eye contact with Peter. Never once did he pause to breathe. His entire spiel came out in one long, clear authoritarian rush.

"That is very good to know, Mr....?" Peter said, pausing for the answer he expected.

"Don't be foolish. Lerner. You knew that. Walter is my son. I am Henry Lerner."

"So that would make the practice Lerner and Son?"

"Walter said you were a smartass. And it would, although I retired from practice three years ago. You can call me Your Honor."

"How many cases does Sonny Lerner bring before Daddy's bench? And how often does he lose?"

"More often than you think. You are a smartass but my son is a prick. I hate the little bastard. But we weren't talking about him."

"No, we weren't talking at all. You came over here and starting spouting some *X-Files* bullshit about the difference between leaving and disappearing. What are we talking about, Judge?"

"Josh Sebold."

"Ah, you know him? No one else seems to remember the poor fellow."

"Of course not. That is perhaps the biggest difference between leaving and disappearing. If you leave, folks will always wonder how you are doing. If you disappear, folks will forget you pretty quick."

"Like you never existed," Peter said, intoning a bit of Boris Karloff.

"While I see you still think this is a joke, I assure you, Mr. Toombs, it is not. You'd do well to remember that. Before you are forgotten." Judge Lerner took one step away from the table then turned for the door. He was gone before Peter could say another word. *Like father, like son*, Peter thought. *They both need to have the last word. I'd hate to be Mrs.*

Lerner. Either one of them.

Peter finished his cheeseburger before he thought to follow the judge to find out what he knew about the missing Josh Sebold. He went to the phone booth near the door to look for the address to the Lerner law practice or better a home number for Judge Lerner. Neither he nor his son were listed but he did get an address for the practice. It was in Provo, a good 40 miles away. He jotted the number down anyway. Peter hadn't prank called anyone in years and it was never too late to start again.

He paid his check, leaving Penny a little extra tip despite her reticence at speaking about Josh Sebold. Getting on her good side was a must if Peter ever wanted to find out what really went on in this town.

***

Peter didn't want to go back home right away but he didn't feel like spending eight hours in town before his meeting with Ben Hill. What he wanted to do was spend some time in the cemetery, talking to Diana. Maybe he'd tell her about the dream he had and ask what she thought about it. Maybe he'd ask her why she hadn't shown up in any of his dreams. He thought it odd that someone he spent so much time thinking about would be completely absent from his dreams. If he closed his eyes (and sometimes even if he didn't) Diana appeared to him as she had been when they first met. He remembered her as she was that prom night, both before and after. He returned to her as she was in the hospital, crying and not wanting to be touched. He could see her as she had been when they'd broken up, walking away into a fate and destiny that ended in her death due to a brain tumor. And the first and latest image: Diana laid out in her coffin, calla lilies surrounding her. He didn't like seeing her like that; the image of her in the casket never resonated with the dense reality of the other images. Even the break-up vision was preferable to the funeral vision.

He walked halfway to the cemetery thinking these thoughts. The images of Diana at different stages all gelled into one overall image, even the last one. The profile of her stone poked out even from the gates. No sentry stood guard. He did a slow 360, looking for any signs of the dishonor guard. No one.

He didn't have the feeling of being watched, the sense of eyes boring through his back, that he felt every other time he came within fifty yards of the cemetery gates. Perhaps this was his chance at spending time with Diana. And if he was caught again, so what? What could they really do to him?

Peter slowly walked into the graveyard confines. He kept looking around, awaiting the eyes he knew would soon scope him out. He reached the northwest quadrant without feeling anything other than built up paranoia. He sprinted the few yards to Diana's plot. Someone was bound to drive by and see him here. He would enjoy the time he was given, for whatever reason it was given.

Nothing had changed here. The same smarmy epitaph, the same portrait. Diana was still dead and not telling any tales. The grass still had not come in and clumps of dirt surrounded the base of her marker. Peter leaned down to touch the stone. He put one hand on the ground, on what he took to be a clump of dirt.

The dirt, it turned out, was a rectangle of dirty brown leather. Having carried something similar in his back pocket for ten years, he knew a wallet when he felt it. On his knees, Peter picked up the wallet and opened it. There was no money and no credit cards, just a driver's license.

Josh Sebold's driver's license.

With the wallet in hand, Peter ran back to his house. He would stay there until eight o'clock, when he would leave to meet Ben. He wasn't sure if he would show Ben the wallet or not but they definitely had something to talk about now.

CHAPTER

~15~

The little red light on his answering machine blinked slowly. Peter hit the button with his left index finger. He still held Sebold's wallet in his right hand. The first message was from the real estate agent, asking if Peter found everything to his satisfaction so far and to call if he needed anything. Great service. That was the first he'd heard from the agent since moving in.

The second message was from Penny at the diner, reminding him that they would be closed the following three days so that Penny could visit her sister in Logan. She wanted to tell him during his lunch, but, well, you know how things can get before a vacation. Even a short one. Peter wasn't sure if Penny was lying about the trip or not. He knew the rest of the crew could handle the townies that might come in. Bern did most of its business during ski season and July was definitely not ski season. She must have her reasons for not wanting him there for a couple days. Peter just wished she could have told him to his face. So much for the extra tip.

The third call had come from the Judge's son, Walter Lerner. Peter had to play it a second time just to be sure he'd heard what he heard.

"Mr. Toombs, good afternoon. You might find Bern a bit lonely for the next few days. I suggest that you stay home.

53

Don't leave your house for anything, not even your daily walks past the cemetery.

"You may be tempted to take this as an opportunity to visit the grave of your so-called beloved. I hope that the item you found there today would discourage you from such actions. Good day, Mr. Toombs."

Walter Lerner knew about the wallet. Peter hadn't felt spied upon, but that didn't mean that young Lerner wouldn't know what he was doing. Especially if the wallet was left there specifically for Peter to find.

Don't be an idiot, Peter told himself. Of course the wallet was left there for him. There were no coincidences. No one just leaves town without everyone else knowing.

Shit.

Peter was now sure that Ben Hill would see the wallet. He was also sure that Ben would tell him the store would be closed for three days. And then the town would be resurrected anew.

Peter changed his clothes, finally relinquishing the wallet in order to do so. He put on black jeans and a black T-shirt. He grabbed his long, black coat from the closet and draped it over his chair in front of the TV. The wallet went into the inside pocket. He had a moment when he wished he still packed a pocketknife. He sat in the chair, turned on his show and watched his friend Connor Parrish tell him to be prepared for the worst in gut-wrenching terror and blood-curdling suspense.

"If you only knew, Connor," Peter said to the screen. "If you only knew how right you were. Later, buddy." He shut his eyes, his arms crossed over his chest and mentally prepared himself for every possibility he could think of. As with any horror writer worth his salt, most of those possibilities were not pleasant.

He opened his eyes when Connor came back on to close the show. Roughly an hour had gone by. Peter's arms were still folded and starting to cramp. He stretched his arms out in front of him, blocking Connor's face with his hands. He needed every inch of his mind and body to be in top form. Which wasn't saying much. Peter, who'd always been a big guy, was sporting a bit of a gut these days. All the walking solidified his calves and thighs but did nothing for his belly. Add the fact that he'd not been in a fight since the one that landed him in detention when he was 15 and Peter Toombs was not what one would expect from a hero.

The heroes of his own books looked a lot like he did and they managed to do heroic things. Then again, they both died in the end, but that was usually what happened to real heroes. Those heroes were Hollywood-ed up for the series and even they didn't all make it to Connor's epilogue alive. Peter, for all intents and purposes, was sure he would die. If not that night then definitely within the next three days.

Worst of all, it appeared that no one would be around to see it.

CHAPTER
~16~

Peter was wrong. It was not his day to die. The same could not be said for Ben Hill. He was still alive and ready to talk when Peter arrived at the bookstore shortly after 8:30 PM. By 9:00, just before the raven cried out the hour, Ben Hill had taken his last breath.

"Thank you for coming, Peter. After our previous conversation, I'd hoped to see you more."

"Yeah, well, let's just say that your town has an odd way of making a guy feel at home."

"After what I have to tell you, you will understand why I will refuse the claim of 'my town.'"

"OK, then. Get to it."

"Right, well..." Ben hesitated for the first time that night. He'd spent the day preparing for this moment and now it seemed that all his preparation had done him little good. "How to go about this, Peter. I never thought I'd be telling anyone these things."

"One word at a time, Ben. One word at a time." A certain calm had come over Peter since entering the small store. He had prepared to be furious with Ben, not conciliatory. Perhaps the calm came from his acceptance of his impending death, whether or not it came tonight. Perhaps it was from the dread fear that whatever Ben would tell him, would get him no closer to Diana than he was this morning. Whatever it was, Peter was not throttling Ben as he'd pictured doing on his way here.

"You're right. Just out with it. That's the best way," Ben said after a few deep inhalations and a quick swipe at the sweat beading his brow. "I have reason to believe that Diana is not in the grave you so desperately wish to visit."

"Excuse me?" Peter said. He should have seen that coming. Peter Toombs? Your table for one is ready. Burgess Meredith will be your waiter. Thank you for dining … in *The Twilight Zone*.

"Now I didn't say she wasn't deceased. That I believe is true. Dear girl. So young. However, if you were to exhume her coffin, you would not find her there. Instead, you would find—" Ben stopped and moved his head to look out his front window. Fright flashed across his face and was gone as quickly as it went.

"What? What did you see?" Peter turned to look but saw only the blackness of night. With Ben's store residing mid-block, neither of the corner streetlights provided much illumination.

"Nothing, nothing. Where was I? Oh yes. Inside that box you would find it…"

Empty. That was the word on Ben's lips as the window shattered and a bullet hit his shoulder. Before Peter could react another bullet whizzed by his ear and entered Ben's forehead, just above his left eye.

Unsure of whether the shots were meant for him or not, Peter ducked, then flattened himself on the floor. The clock-raven began cawing; Ben Hill was silent. While the entrance wounds Peter could see sprayed blood, he knew that the exit wounds he couldn't see would be worse. Not spraying blood, just suddenly empty like when the bottom of a grocery bag tears. One second, it's holding your brain and the next, your brain is all over the floor.

Peter, ever the observer, took it in. How the pools of blood spread out from Ben's body, reaching for the shelves of Best Sellers and New Releases. How white flecks of skull mixed with strands of hair and brain on the covers of books Of Local Interest. On that shelf, behind a smear of scalp, was a copy of *Takes My Life*. A placard that had read "Local Author" was so covered in blood that it now read "Lo l uth". Peter saw all of this with two separate eyes: One that saw just how close to the death he'd predicted for himself he had actually come; The second that saw how wrong he'd been with a few of the death scenes he'd written. There were no last words, no final warning. He'd barely heard the glass shattering even though shards of it poked out of the back of his coat. He'd heard the second bullet buzz by his ear. He heard Ben hit the floor. And he saw that last word forming on Ben's lips, ready to be spoken aloud.

Empty. Ben Hill, who could now be chased by scantily clad young ladies in heaven, believed that Diana's coffin was empty. How could that be? Ben had seen her body inside the casket. He had seen them lower it into the plot at the Bern Cemetery. He had seen them close the lid after the viewing. He had...

No, wait. He hadn't seen anyone close the lid. He had been outside in the snow. He'd been craving his last cigarette and howling in the wind. He hadn't seen anything. But there couldn't have been time. Not with all those people there. No one could have taken Diana's body out of its final resting-place and then wheeled the empty box into the chapel area without someone knowing about it. Someone had to know. David, maybe? Or Aaron? Absolutely. Aaron Doyle would know whether or not his wife was really buried in the Bern Cemetery.

Peter stayed down on the floor well after the raven had stopped cawing. He thought about how he would contact Aaron Doyle and what he would say. He thought about staying alive until he knew what was going on, why someone would want to kill an old man like Ben Hill. He thought, as always, about Diana and a little about Kurt. Ben, apparently, did not bleed Dodger Blue. He didn't dodge well at all.

He didn't think about how those two bullets were probably meant for him. He'd forgotten, again, about Josh Sebold and the wallet in his coat pocket. He didn't think about how he would get out of the store and back home.

At least, not until he'd heard the raven call out the ten o'clock hour and then eleven o'clock. He did think that being in a room with a dead body at midnight, a mechanical raven crying down the dark for its former owner, was a little too creepy. Even for him.

Just before midnight, closer than he knew, Peter Toombs raised himself up on his hands and knees, not minding the broken glass, and crawled out of the Bern Bookseller. He really wanted to believe that things could not get worse, but knew, with all those possibilities, that things most likely would.

CHAPTER

~17~

He crawled like that, keeping close to the ground and next to the buildings, for three blocks. He hid in doorways and stayed out of what little light there was. After three blocks, Peter decided he could stand up in relative safety. He took off his coat and plucked out shards of glass. He reached behind him and drew his fingers away with very little blood on them. *Good coat*, he thought. And people used to make fun of him for wearing it during the middle of summer. Shows them. *If whoever makes long black coats needs a spokesperson, I am there.*

Peter continually looked over his shoulder the entire walk home. He didn't see a single person. Nor did he see a car, either one moving or one parked on the street. He didn't see a light on anywhere. True, it was midnight and small towns sleep early, but there are usually one or two night owls, a local cop, or at least an insomniac. The whole town couldn't have gone to Logan to visit Penny's sister. Could they?

There was still one person in town. Or had been at nine o'clock this evening. Peter didn't hear the sounds of a get-away car but considering his own crawl-and-walk home, it wasn't out of the question for the shooter to have simply walked away. Perhaps the person had come down to the obliterated window and seen all that blood and two bodies lying on the floor and assumed the job was done. Two shots, two kills. No witnesses. Maybe the shooter had seen from his roost both Ben and Peter fall and assumed he was a better shot than Lee Harvey and went on his merry way.

Perhaps shit, Peter thought. *That bastard is here somewhere and if he thinks he can pull the trigger on Peter Toombs, he has another thing coming.* Whatever thing that might be would have to wait for morning. Peter's knees and hands were killing him now. Crawl a mile on another man's knees and know how he dies. Peter reminded himself to write that down when he got home.

***

There are some men who court Death and taunt it. Peter Toombs was a first-rate taunter. After having been vaguely threatened and then nearly shot in the same day, Peter could not help but laugh at the image of Death he held in his head. Thankfully, he did not laugh out loud. If he had, the shooter would have had him without having to take a second look. While Peter first crawled, then walked, toward his home, Josh Sebold loaded two more rounds in his .223 rifle to replace those he had dispensed with. After seeing both men in the bookstore go down, he sincerely thought he had done his job. If Peter had risen to his knees any sooner or made the slightest noise on his way out of the bookstore, Sebold would have heard him and ended him.

If Peter knew how lucky he was, perhaps he would be thanking God for a change instead of swearing at Him.

CHAPTER
~18~

The cemetery has always been on his way home. Tonight, though, Peter didn't really want to walk by it. As he was plotting a course to his house that would circumvent the cemetery, he found himself standing at its very gates. There were no streetlights on this section of road, no houses, no businesses. Even the stars seemed to have been shut off for the night. The sliver of moon hanging above the hills did little to compensate for this lack of light.

True, dark midnight, now well after one o'clock. A witches' hour if there ever was one. Peter gazed deep into the graveyard. He knew where to look to see Diana's headstone. He knew it was too dark to see it but his overactive imagination helped him place a memory of seeing the marker in bright daylight over the unforgiving darkness. Yes, there it was. "Daughter, Sister, Wife, Friend" catching the sun, leftover drops of sprinkler water sparkling like lost diamonds on the surface. One drop running down the face in the portrait, making it look like Diana was crying.

She would be, Peter thought, if she knew her final wishes had not been fulfilled. That despite the beautiful memorial placed there, her own body, sick as it had become, was not there. There was only one way to be sure if she was there or not. The splinters of glass, pushed deeper from

63

crawling over a concrete sidewalk, screamed at Peter. We can't operate a shovel, Peter, not tonight. Let us rest. If she's in there, she isn't going anywhere. If she's not, well, a few more hours won't change that. Please, let us rest.

He lifted his eyes to the sky and the fingernail moon for advice. In the non-light, he could make out a darker shape against the canvas of night. An owl, circling the cemetery, hooted down at him. The language of owls seemed sad to Peter, a melancholy diatribe against all things that happen during the day. Whether the cry was in sorrow for Peter's battered hands or for Diana, he did not know. He pulled his coat tighter around him and continued walking home.

Peter arrived home without further incident. No one shot at him; no owls followed him home. No visions of undead ex-girlfriends or unborn children. The house stood on its hill as silent and unrelenting as the first day Peter had come there. At first, the house had seemed like home, a place he was meant to be. Tonight, it felt like just one more stop on the way to the grave. When he left that evening, he did not think he would ever be back inside this house again. He had come very close to being right. The house, he felt, had given him up for dead, as well.

He wasn't dead and had promised himself that he would not go down easily and without knowing exactly what had happened to Diana. Ben Hill was dead and Josh Sebold was missing and likely dead (as far as he knew). Judge Lerner was crazy and his son very much following in Daddy's loony footsteps. Penny at the diner had deserted him. He had none of his own family to call for support.

Peter showered and wrapped his hands. The injuries were not close to serious. Besides, he would get help for the digging. He would go to bed and in the morning he would call David.

And then he would call Aaron.

Sleep did not come as quickly as he'd hoped it would.

Peter traditionally slept flat on his back. The little pinpricks of glass that had penetrated both his coat and his shirt would not allow Peter to sleep in his usual way. He turned on his side, facing the wall. He began to recite poetry to put himself to sleep. After one stanza of Emily Dickinson, Peter was fast asleep.

CHAPTER
~19~

Back in Dodger Stadium again. Peter could see the Giants in the visitors' dugout but he didn't mind. He knew they were his own heart and as long as they were there, his heart still beat. Can't kill me that easy, he thought. The pre-game ceremonies were still going, some Hollywood star murdering the National Anthem.

He looked to his left, expecting to see the seven-year-old version of Kurt. He was there, now wearing his own jersey, a number 10 Sciocsia jersey, and the cap that Peter had bought him last dream. Kurt smiled at Peter and slammed a fist into the mitt he wore. They hadn't caught a foul ball yet, but it was only a matter of time and one must always be prepared.

Peter looked to his right and saw an empty seat. It was the only empty seat in the entire stadium. Turning back to Kurt, he asked, "Who is sitting here, son?"

"Mom went to get the Dodger Dogs, Dad. Don't worry, she'll be back."

"For you," Peter said.

"What? No, she's getting dogs for all of us. She didn't want us to miss the first pitch. Some actor guy is throwing out the first pitch today. Mom said you knew him. Some guy named... Connor Parrish." Kurt had to look at his program to remember the name. "Do you, Dad? Do you know him?"

"Yeah, son. I do."

"That's so cool."

The Hollywood-type finished butchering the last few bars of "The Star-Spangled Banner" amidst a cacophony of cheers and boos. Connor came out of the dugout wearing a custom jersey: Parrish 13. He waved to the crowd and pointed right at Peter and Kurt. Peter waved back and Kurt started jumping up and down, hollering for Connor to put it right across the plate.

The man sitting in front of Kurt craned his head around and yelled at Kurt. "Sit down, you little shit. The game hasn't even started yet."

"My daddy knows that guy, mister," Kurt replied. Peter looked at the man and watched his face morph from the indistinguishable features of a dream-extra into someone he almost recognized.

"Yeah, well, he knows me, too and look what that got me." The face, or what was left of it anyway, gelled into the face of Ben Hill. Kurt quieted down and Ben turned back to the diamond. Peter could see the backs of Ben's eyes through the exit wound. Just as he was reaching out to Ben, to apologize, a hand dropped on his shoulder

"Peter, is something wrong?" It was Diana, making her first appearance in his dreams since well before her death. She held a tray of Dodger Dogs and was smiling at him like everything in the world really was OK. Just another day at the ball field.

"No, baby, nothing wrong. Just thought I saw someone else I knew." Peter smiled back and helped her with the hotdogs.

"OK. Did you see your friend down there? He looked well." Diana sat in her seat on his right. Kurt to his left. The recently deceased Ben Hill in front of him. There was something there, he thought. He couldn't grasp the idea yet, but it would come to him.

"Yeah, old Connor down there," Peter said. "I'm surprised anyone recognizes him without his mask on." Diana laughed at the joke and put her arm around his shoulders, then kissed him on the cheek. This is how things should have turned out: a baseball game with my wife and my son; my best friend down on the field, hobnobbing with Major Leaguers.

And then it hit him. Diana, Kurt, Ben. If he looked around, he was sure he would see the faces of more people he knew were dead. Something had happened to Connor. That was why Leslie, his agent had called. Something was wrong with Connor and they wanted Peter back to do the hosting job he had wanted to begin with.

But that wasn't the worst part. Connor might still be alive, just in trouble. He was on the field not in the stands. As Peter watched faces flash across the big screen, confirming his theory about tonight's special crowd, he saw a face he did not want to see among the thousands in attendance.

He saw the face of David Ward, Diana's brother.

CHAPTER
~20~

Seeing David in the dream did not automatically mean that David was dead. Peter was in the dream and, although it had been close, he wasn't dead. He was alive and well, maybe a little frazzled after nearly being shot and having to crawl a portion of his way home. But alive. The pain in his hands and his back told him that. The dead do not feel pain.

Or do they? Peter thought. Why else would there be ghosts if not for pain? Pain and suffering did not require a physical body. If it did, Hell would not exist. And even if you still had your body, no bodily harm had to be present to induce pain. When Diana lost the baby, Peter felt pain. When Diana died, he felt pain. It hurt in his gut and his heart. It hurt his eyes when he cried too much. The palms of his hands would hurt from the digging his nails into them. To varying degrees, these were pains he felt every day.

So he knew he was alive but what about David? It had taken Diana six months after her passing to show up in the dream, any dream. For all Peter knew David could have been dead for months or minutes. Was it that distance, the not knowing for sure, the reason David had a seat on the other side of the stadium? He knew David for longer than he knew Ben Hill but Ben sat right in front of him. Then again, whatever may or may not have happened to David, Peter hadn't been there. Ben Hill's blood, not to mention some of his brain and skull, had been on Peter. Peter was absolutely positive that Ben Hill was dead. No such assurance concerning David Ward.

As he was flipping the pages of his address book for David's phone number in Blackhawk, Peter thought of a face he didn't see among the dead that he should have. He did not see Josh Sebold anywhere, not even in the nosebleed seats. So did that mean Sebold wasn't dead? If Lerner hadn't been talking about Peter finding the wallet and the threat that came with it, what had he been talking about? There was an explanation and he would think about it later. First, he had to call David.

Peter dialed the number and held his breath through four rings before it was answered by an unfamiliar voice.

"Hi, my name is Peter Toombs, an old friend of David's. May I speak with him, please?" Peter said, using his interview voice.

"What is this in regards to, Mr. Toombs?" replied the hostile female voice.

"Nothing. Just felt like calling and seeing how he was doing. Catch up on old times, you know." It all sounded fake. Even the part that was true about wanting to see how he was doing.

"This is his fiancée and I'm afraid you can't talk to him," she said, her voice losing its stoicism. "David was in an accident yesterday and Debbie is missing."

Peter's first impulse was to ask a million questions and to ask only one question. He knew the answer to his one question.

"There is someone here who would like to speak with you, Mr. Toombs. Here he is." Peter was afraid that it would be David and Diana's father, a man who had never quite warmed up to him. If it was Aaron Doyle, it would save Peter another call. It was neither.

"Mr. Toombs, my name is Raines. Sergeant Raines of the Blackhawk P.D.," said a man with less passion than David's fiancée had answered with. He definitely sounded like a cop. "Where exactly are you calling from, if you'd be so kind." *I already know, he meant, so don't bother lying.*

"From my house in Bern," Peter said, trying to affect as much standoffishness as he had received.

"That would be the home once occupied by the Ward family, correct?"

"Yes it would, why?"

"Mr. Toombs, where were you yesterday and last night, say until about 1 AM?"

I was being threatened and ignored most of the morning. Later I was in the presence of a man who had his skull blown out all over the Best Sellers shelf. "I was here in town all day. Back and forth between the shops and home."

"And there are witnesses to this?"

"Yes… " *but none of them are available. You see, one of them is dead, the rest of the town has closed for the next few days to visit Penny's family in Logan. Except for a man I thought was dead who might actually be the man who nearly killed me.*

"Would any of them swear to seeing you there?"

"Sergeant, I'm not exactly well-liked here in town. I honestly don't know what they would say." *The truth feels good, doesn't it?*

"You aren't exactly a saint to the Wards, either," Raines said.

No shit, Sergeant Sherlock, Peter thought.

"You had a history with their daughter, correct? A Mrs. Diana Ward Doyle, deceased?"

"Our relationship ended well before she became deceased." *Dammit, Peter. Don't let this guy bait you into making those smartass comments.*

"So I understand. Have you had any recent contact

with any member of the family? In particular David or Debbie?"

"Not since Diana's funeral."

"Will you be available by phone for the remainder of the day? In case I have more questions for you? Or if you hear from Debbie?" You'll be available, or I'll be there with a squad car just as soon as I can.

"Yes, but if the line is busy, it is because I'm speaking with my lawyer."

"That, Mr. Toombs, might be a good idea." Sergeant Raines hung up on Peter before Peter could hang up on him.

The call confirmed for Peter that, if David was not dead, he certainly was close to it. What Peter did not expect was this cop, Raines, implying that he was somehow involved in whatever had happened to David. If Raines caught a bug and showed up in Bern and saw the entire town deserted except for Peter, what would he think then? What if the first things he saw were the shattered bookstore window and the body rotting on the floor? He would see the tracks Peter left while crawling on his hands and knees. He would see where those tracks ended and footprints began. He would follow those prints right to Peter's front door.

Peter, after literally dodging a bullet the night before, was once again in deep shit.

No reprieve, is there? Three days would be great but how about three hours. Three waking hours with nothing going on in my head to fuck up the time. A clear, blue-sky day to contemplate nothing. Not Diana, not Kurt. And now add not David. Please, God, let me be.

He was crying again, this time for his lost friend. The one person close to Diana who still liked him. He couldn't help but think David's death had a connection to whatever the hell was going on in Bern. After all, Peter only knew of three people that had been in Bern throughout the day and night: himself, the dearly departed Ben Hill, and the apparently still kicking and gunning Josh Sebold. It had to be Sebold, he was sure of it now.

Three people, Sergeant. Anyone else who lives here could be anywhere and could have done anything. Do I know where they went? Well, according to a Judge I met, no one here leaves without telling someone where they are going. Unless they all disappeared. But if they are gone long enough, we'll forget about them. Sure as shit we will.

Peter scanned the pages of his address book again, noting the page with Aaron Doyle's phone number on it for later use and, instead of calling his lawyer, he called Connor Parrish.

CHAPTER
~21~

Connor Parrish was fairly famous among a certain crowd well before he ever met Peter Toombs. He'd done more than his share of low budget horror movies, first as a victim and later as a villain. But donning the mask of "Lord Cadaver" in the horror franchise *Lord of Death* got Connor his big break. Five films over ten years followed before Connor was replaced by a younger actor in the film *Lord of Death VI: Kid Cadaver*. As Connor had expected, the film flopped. Instead of bringing him back, the studio decided they'd had enough of *Lord of Death*.

When Connor was introduced to Peter for the first time, Connor was almost a has-been and Peter was a wannabe with one novel and a bunch of short stories. Peter still thought of Connor as an icon and had gratuitously flashed the "Cadaver Court Fan Club" card he kept in his wallet. Connor, happy to meet a dedicated fan, signed the card and a photo but thought no more of it until later at the convention.

That night, one of the presentations was a panel of up-and-coming horror writers. Connor recognized none of the names on the bill and had voiced aloud for anyone to hear that he was sure "Peter Toombs" must be a pseudonym. He peeked inside and saw the young man he'd given an autograph to approaching the podium. When a woman on the front row passed out after only a few paragraphs, Connor took a seat.

And then, three years later, Connor was hosting the show that Peter created. With the horror boom occurring in the early twenty-first century, both Peter and Connor seemed to be on top. But less than a year later, Peter was off the show and Connor was tired. He knew he'd never win an Oscar and that was fine. He knew that if he quit, the fountain of young starlets would dry up. That was fine, too; remember, Connor was tired.

It was he who convinced the producers to do what they could to get Peter back. The show was disintegrating under the pens of sloppy writers. The current writing staff included three men and two women whose only screenwriting credits were a combined seven remakes of either old TV shows or classic horror films. Sadly, Connor thought, those movies kept making money, which meant similar projects would continue to be made. Which meant that the writers of those absurdities would continue to get jobs. It pissed Connor off to no end. He never wanted Peter to leave in the first place. When Peter began *Graveyard Paradise* it was original and edgy. And he wrote the entire season himself. Twenty-six one-hour episodes, plus all of Connor's introductions and "Famous Last Words," as he liked to call them. Seasons Two and Three had seen nineteen different writers, including the current Fab Five, try their hand at replacing Peter Toombs. While there had been some good shows (like "A51", the one about a little town on the edge of Area 51 and "Voices Carry", about a journalist who spends a night in the home of a murder-suicide, just to name two), they were all based on outlines or stories Peter had left them. Nothing good and nothing original had come from anyone working on the show since Peter left. If Peter did not come back, the cable channel paying for the whole mess would drop the axe.

The catch was, and Connor knew it better than

anyone, was that Peter wanted to be the host. If that was what it took for *Graveyard Paradise* to be a great show again, then that was how it had to be. If Connor had to leave, then so be it. If, by some chance, Peter no longer wanted to host but was willing to write and produce the show again, with Connor firmly seated in the host's (electric) chair, then so be it. Then again, if Peter wanted nothing to do with the show anymore, well, shit. It had been a good run from the top to the bottom.

Either way, Connor would never have to suffer the dregs of the current writers again. He'd never have to listen to a conversation about how remaking *Welcome Back, Kotter* with John Travolta as Mr. Kotter was a great idea. Never again would he listen to some punk tell him that the modern versions of *The Texas Chainsaw Massacre* and *Dawn of the Dead* were far superior to the originals. Peter was a true fan, Connor knew. While certain remakes had their moments, none could touch the brutality and rawness of their forerunners.

To do something original, acknowledging those forerunners and continuing on with what he saw as their grander vision, that was what Peter wanted. With Connor he'd gone to Italy to watch *giallo*. They'd gone to Japan to see firsthand the horror movement going on there. Together they endured film festivals in Spain and Canada. They'd seen that Peter was not the only one trying to recapture the grandeur of the 1930s and 1970s horror films at the same time. They met people who would help them garner studio contacts. They met actors and directors that would help bring Peter's sick visions to life.

And after Peter left, so did they. Not all at once, no. Other offers came in as they were bound to based on Season One's overwhelming success. Whomever replaced someone who'd left never seemed quite as talented, quite as competent. Only Connor was left now.

***

Connor spilled his coffee when he heard Peter's voice on the phone. There he'd been, thinking of his friend, hoping said friend would once again become a work partner, when he answered the phone. Even in the heart of a professional scaremonger hope dies hard.

"Connor, glad I caught you," Peter said, instead of "Hello."

"Peter, good to hear your voice," Connor said, although he was not at all sure how good Peter's voice actually sounded. He must not be taking the job. Shit.

"Yeah, you too. Look, I just needed to hear you talk for a second. I'm so happy you answered."

"Well, you found me at my coffee, so no one else is around to answer. Is something bothering you, Peter? I mean, we haven't talked for quite some time. You aren't exactly the kind of guy who calls someone out of the blue. Does this have anything to do with Leslie calling you the other day?"

"Leslie? Oh shit, right. About coming back. Listen, I'd like to, but this isn't a good time for me, you know? I'm going through some things you might not understand. I'll tell you all about it soon. We'll sit in that coffeehouse in Glendale you like and I'll spill my guts. But not right now. I just had to make sure you weren't…"

"Weren't what, Peter?"

"Dead. I had to make sure you weren't dead." Peter hung up.

Connor held onto his silent phone for a good two minutes before softly setting it back in its cradle. *Dead?* he thought. *Why would I be dead?* Although a day of shooting on *Graveyard Paradise* had been scheduled, Connor knew it wouldn't matter. The show was dead and Connor wasn't. Now he had to go to his friend and find out why that mattered so much all of a sudden.

By three o'clock that afternoon, Connor Parrish was on a plane to Salt Lake City with a rental car confirmation in one pocket and a map of Utah in the other.

Around the same time, Peter was being questioned by Sergeant Raines concerning his involvement in the death of David Ward and the disappearance of Debbie Ward.

CHAPTER

~22~

Connor was OK for now. Peter recalled the last dream; Connor had been on the field not in the stands. With the sun streaming through the front window, the thought that something could have happened to Connor seemed nearly ridiculous. But, he reminded himself, David was dead, so the notion that Connor might at least be in trouble would not disappear. Last night's events were just as absurd but he had his hands and back to dissuade him from dismissing the fact of those events.

Peter sat by the phone, whether or not to call his lawyer. Whether or not to call Aaron Doyle as he had originally planned. First, a walk. A walk would do him good. *No one would try to shoot me in the middle of the day*, he thought.

He went the way that he'd used to come home after the shooting. He did his best to walk on his own footprints; a paranoid thing to do but he did it anyway. That was his excuse: cover up my tracks. The other reason for taking the long way was to avoid the cemetery. He didn't know if the Bern townsfolk would be there or not. He pictured them piling up wood for whatever bizarre rituals they would perform over the course of their three-day bacchanal. Whatever dark Sabbath they had planned, Peter wanted none of it. The residents didn't want him involved. Lerner the younger had told him to stay home.

Here he was, though, walking back into town. He half-expected it to be empty. His other half expected to be shown a deserted town only to have everyone jump out and laugh at the silly joke the played on the new guy. Ha-ha, guys. You treat everyone new like this or just me? Payback's a bitch, especially when it comes to practical jokes.

What happened to Ben was no joke. Even the best special effects guys in Hollywood would need at least two takes to pull off something like that. Most of them went out of their way to make sure no one was hurt, too. Kidding aside, Ben was dead.

The real joke, one almost as not-funny as watching Ben's skull explode, was seeing the front window of the Bern Bookseller right where it always had been. The big gold letters clearly spelling out the name of the place, with "Ben Hill, Prop." beneath just like the first day Peter saw it.

So maybe last night didn't happen. There was no one around to ask. No one jumped out to say boo, yet. *This is as far from funny as one can get*, Peter thought.

He pressed his head against the window and discovered that he was not crazy. Ben's body was gone, as were the books that had absorbed the flying parts of him. Right below the window, however, shards of broken glass glittered in the mid-morning sun.

For the second time in two days, Peter Toombs ran home. It was better than crawling.

Peter ran so fast that he didn't notice that he went his usual way, past the cemetery. He didn't see Judge Lerner standing in the center, watching him run like a scared little kid. He didn't see Walter Lerner or Penny or even Helga standing with all the other townspeople on the far edge of the graveyard, equally enamored with Peter's mad sprint for home. Nor did he see the body of Ben Hill leaning against the one tree within the funereal borders. If he had seen what remained of Ben there, he might also have followed Ben's soulless gaze up the tree to watch the feet of Josh Sebold swaying in the breeze. Sebold hung there, only dead since breakfast, with a sign pinned to his shirt. "Nice shootin, Tex," was written on the piece of paper in something that looked like blood and ink mixed.

If Peter had seen this, he would have identified the color of the substance as Dodger Blue.

CHAPTER

~23~

Peter grabbed his good suitcase and filled it with clothes. He filled his duffle bag with socks and underwear. He even took the seven bottles of Smirnoff Ice from the refrigerator and put them in a mini-cooler. He set these three bags by the door and went to get his laptop. He could worry about food and shelter later. Clothing, booze and his computer: these things mattered the most to him. He would spend the next three days in the woods somewhere or drive into Provo and take a hotel room for a while. Then he would come back, box up a few more things and then get the hell out of Bern.

Not a perfect plan, he knew. At the moment, however, it was the best he could come up with. How much stuff did he need? He'd come back for his books and movies and CDs. His clothes, of course, would go; all those black T-shirts with rude things written on them. What else? Nothing.

His memories of Diana would have to stay here, too. If he couldn't leave them behind, he would always be chasing her. Always wondering if Ben Hill had been right about where her body did not lie. Much as the last few years after she'd left him had been, in fact. Truly, it was no way to live. Peter had known it for a very long time. Still, he came to Bern to attempt some sort of closure, to see if Essie's funeral prophecy would come true. Would Diana come back for him? Right now, for the first time since looking into Essie's blue eyes, Peter did not care. He wanted to get the fuck out of Bern. Leaving Diana behind, in whatever form she had, would be the best for Peter.

So there it was; Peter was finally over his lost love, Diana. He could leave this house he'd bought simply to be closer to her. He could leave the crazy little town she loved. He could go somewhere with no connections to Diana, somewhere he'd never have to see a picture of her, or hear her voice, or...

The cassette Diana sent him would have to stay here, too. But first Peter had to find it. That tape had a funny way of popping up at the least inopportune times. Like the time Peter had one of the actresses from *Graveyard Paradise* in his temporary Hollywood apartment and she wanted to listen to something new. She had been intrigued by the unmarked cassette and put it in the stereo. The sound of Diana's voice had filled the room. The actress had not stayed much longer.

So where, now, was the stupid thing? Peter could never find it when he wanted it. He couldn't count all the times he'd meant to throw the damn thing in the trash or to record over it or to just plain destroy it. Pull the tape out of the casing and light it on fire. If he could find it, he had trouble not listening to it one last time before ending the existence of the blasted thing.

Not this time, bucko. This time, he would tear the thin tape right from its shell without even thinking about it.

The stereo contained a tape already, so he hit PLAY to see what he had been listening to. It was, to his limited surprise, the tape Diana had sent him shortly before her death.

"...still get double vision sometimes so I haven't read your book yet, but thank you for..."

Peter pushed STOP. He meant to push EJECT but

his finger landed on REWIND instead. *Fortune's Fool*, he thought as the tape rewound to its beginning. I am Fortune's Fool.

When the tape stopped rewinding, Peter pushed PLAY and readied himself for another bout of crying.

CHAPTER
~24~

Hi, hello, it's me, Diana, but you probably knew that. This is the second time I've made a tape like this. The first time didn't go very well. I have days that are great and days that aren't so great. Today is a good day. Aaron wonders why I'm using one of my good days to do this. I've tried to get him to understand, but it's difficult. He thought it so weird that you wrote to him for permission to write to me. I still get double vision sometimes so I haven't read your book yet, but thank for sending it. Double vision also makes it hard to write anything, so I thought a tape would be fine. I hope you can listen to the whole thing and not hate me.

One problem with the tumor and the surgery is that I don't remember some things too well. A lot of stuff from senior year in high school and after that is gone. I'm glad you remember so much. A lot of it went into that first book, I know. When I read that, before the tumor, I wasn't sure if the Diana in the dedication was me or not. About halfway through I knew it was. I'm so sorry things were bad for you.

I've done a lot since then. After leaving Reno, after leaving you, I came back to Salt Lake and did some more school. While you were in New York and California getting famous, I was working in an electronics shop. I spent my days soldering motherboards and things like that. That's where I met Aaron. He's so good to me, I can't believe it.

We dated off and on for a while and when he asked me to

marry him, I nearly died. It was so storybook, you would have puked. If it weren't for the look on his face, I would have laughed. I said yes and we got married not too long afterwards.

I feel bad about not inviting you and some other people. Remember Terry? He died a couple months later. It was just that I didn't want to go to the trouble of tracking people down, finding their addresses, and all that. I guess it hurt a few people, especially you. Of course, it would have been awkward with you there. I had no idea what you might do or what my parents would do. You probably would have just hung out with David and gotten drunk. Or maybe you would have hit on some of my friends. I won't say who was there but I'm sure you'd know who.

And that is one reason why I left you. This is the part I know you've always wondered about. I remember how you tried to date Sarah before you started paying attention to me. I hated knowing I was your second choice. I knew that I'd have to compete with your career once it got going. And I worried that whole summer about losing my spot to the baby. I'm sorry I lost it. I think sometimes that I killed it with negativity. You never thought that, I know, otherwise you would have left me way before I left you. Don't bother lying about it; it is too late for either of us to lie anymore. That is why I left. It was always my choice. If you are going to hate someone, hate me.

You can't do that, can you? You came close in your first book. You killed my character. I knew she'd come back because I know you. You used to have that poster that said, "If you love someone, let them go. If they come back, they are yours forever. If they don't, they never were." I can see you spending so much time sitting in your house hoping for me to come back.

It wasn't just the book, either. All those short stories. The ones about the guy that has to go on after the love of his life dies. He's always so sad. Sometimes even I believed it. Sometimes I thought they were about me. Most of the time, I thought it was Kurt you were lamenting. Maybe it was me, after all. Maybe you thought it was easier to kill me than to let go. I don't know.

You've been shaking your head. You know what you know and

most of the time so do I. I know that I may feel fine right now, but it won't last. There is no guarantee that I will be here tomorrow.

When I had my seizure, Aaron was right there for me. He carried me to the car and into the hospital. He didn't want to leave me when the nurses and doctors told him to. You two are more alike than you know and so very different. Maybe you'll meet him someday. Hopefully I will be there to facilitate. It could be a very good thing or a very bad thing.

I hadn't planned on telling him about the baby or much about you. He was there when I answered a bunch of medical questions about myself. The doctor asked if I'd ever been pregnant. Aaron was right there but I was so scared after the seizure that I told the doctor everything. I didn't know if it would make a difference or not but Aaron would have found out anyway.

He knew I'd been with you. We'd been dating by the time I got Scream Queen. *When it came in the mail, he thought I was in some book club. Your name wasn't on the package, just your publisher or your agent, I can't remember. Then he asked me what kind of club sends out personally autographed copies. He thought your name was fake.*

We read that book together and he promised to read me the next one. Ever thought of audio versions? Don't let some hack actor do it, though. If you can't get Anthony Hopkins to do it, you should do it yourself. Making tapes is easier than I thought it would be. If I can do it, missing a portion of my brain, you certainly could.

OK, yes, there are days when I miss you and wonder what it would have been like if we'd gotten married, whether we had the baby or not. And—strange how I can remember some things and completely forget other things—I remember that we were married, if only for a night. Do you remember?

We went to that dance, was it a Sadie Hawkins? Must have been because I asked you. They had the mock wedding ceremonies with cheap fake rings. We got married. You picked silver rings because neither of us looked good in gold. Plus, we both covered ourselves in silver jewelry. So, yeah, we were married and that was one of the happiest nights of my life.

Then, some other times, I can't stand the thought of you. My parents hate you more, probably for knocking me up. Aaron really hated you after finding that out, too. Your letter to him almost brought him to your side but I think if you met on the street and he recognized you, you might end up in the hospital. Your dust cover photos look exactly how I remember you. Even in black and white, I know it is you.

I don't understand their hate. The reasons they hate you, I've moved on from. I wish I had a baby before the tumor but now I'm glad I don't. How horrible would it be for a child to lose his mother at so young an age? I do understand my hate and it isn't something I can explain. I hate you because I care about you so much. I want you to be successful and happy. You are on your way to success. Happiness, though, I don't know if you ever will be. I don't know that you can be. Maybe if I died, you would be able to let me go. I hate you because you say you love me so much. There have been times, especially after the miscarriage, when I sincerely doubted whether you loved me. And just as many times when I doubted my feelings for you.

If I die from this, which even after one surgery I'm not out of the woods yet, the first person I see in Heaven will be Kurt. I wonder what he'll say to me. Will he ask why he couldn't be born? I don't know. I think his first words to me will be "Where's Daddy?"

It is a good question. Where are you, Peter? I know where I am, although I can't always remember where I've been. And I know where I will end up. I'm going back to Bern. If I see you there, great. If you see me, wait for me. I'll be back.

Goodbye, Peter. A part of me that is here still loves you.

***

The tape kept running, white noise mixed in with various background noises and voices, like Diana forgot to turn the machine off when she was done. Peter let it roll on and on until it came to the end. It caught there for a moment before the player automatically shut off. It was shorter than it seemed when listening to it. Diana frequently paused between paragraphs and sometimes between sentences. It could not have been an easy thing to do. Peter wondered just how the rest of her day went after finishing the tape. He also wondered how long it took her to remember that she forgot to push STOP. He wondered if she knew that Peter heard her husband, Aaron, yell at her for trying to tell Peter she loved him.

Peter also wondered if anyone else ever knew that Aaron had hit her. It was small; more like a slap on the wrist might sound than a slap across the face. Like a sound effect slap, not hand to face but hand to nameless meat product simulating face. If it wasn't for the yelling and the "I'm sorry" afterward, Peter may have doubted that he'd heard a slap at all. What Peter did not know was that that had been the only time during the marriage of Aaron and Diana Doyle that Aaron had hit Diana. But why would he? He only had the one tape to go by.

CHAPTER
~25~

While Peter was listening to Diana's tape in Bern and Connor was boarding a plane at LAX, Aaron Doyle was hearing the latest on David and Debbie from Mr. Ward. Aaron, as Peter had thought all along, was not a bad guy. Peter thought this even after listening to the tape and continued to think such after the funeral. Aaron Doyle was just one of those guys whose luck is either really good or really bad. The day he met Diana at the electronics plant they both worked at began with Aaron finding a five dollar bill next to the gas pump and ended with him calling Diana to set up a date. The week before Diana's first seizure he'd been laid off from the plant due to downsizing.

The day Mark Ward, David and Diana's father called him, Aaron had woken up with a first-rate hangover. When the phone rang at eleven AM, Aaron was in the bathroom of the small apartment in downtown Salt Lake City he'd moved into after Diana died, pissing a river. It took more 3.2 % alcohol beer to get drunk, which meant that a person had to piss more. For Aaron, who'd only been drunk three times before Diana's funeral—his senior prom, his wedding night and the night he'd been laid off—had not yet visited the local State Liquor Agency. Grocery store beer was just fine, even the 30-pack of Natural Light he finished off around one that morning.

He wasn't going to answer the phone until he heard Mark Ward's voice coming from the machine. Even then, hearing what sounded like crying in the background, he was not sure about picking up the handset. He did, and knew it was going to be one of those days.

"David is dead," Mark Ward said, trying to sound as calm as he possibly could. "Hit-and-run while crossing Main Street in Blackhawk. No witnesses at all. And no one has seen Debbie since the day before. We thought she was with him but we just don't know."

"Mr. Ward, I'm so sorry. Do the cops have anything to go on?" Aaron asked, knowing that "no witnesses" meant probably not.

"Yeah. Raines, the town cop, said that a copy of that book Toombs wrote was lying next to him on the ground. He wasn't sure if David had been carrying it, but it was a signed copy, to him and dated yesterday.

"We told him that David and Toombs had been friends and we had to tell him a little bit about Toombs and Diana. He, Raines that is, is going out to Bern to talk to that bastard."

"Why Bern? I thought he lived in Reno," Aaron said, mildly shocked.

"We didn't tell you? My God, I'm sorry. Peter Toombs has been living in Bern for a month or so. He bought our old house."

"The one on the hill?"

"Yes. He knew, as I'm sure you do, that Diana had such fond memories of that house. Of all of Bern."

Aaron knew. He and Diana had themselves spoken of buying the house to have their own children in. They'd only planned on one or two; the house in Bern would last them into their Golden Years. Those Golden Years had been robbed from them by some cruel joke of God. Instead of making babies and living life, Diana was feeding worms and Aaron was pounding brew.

The real joke, that neither Aaron nor Peter knew—maybe Diana did, though—was how alike the thinking of the two men had been. Growing old with Diana in Bern had been the fantastic goal for both men. Blaming God had served as a crutch for each, as well. While these could be seen as crucial faults in the only two men ever to share a bed with Diana Ward, it was also something that tied them together. At least, both men rationalized at separate times, God was paying attention.

That was not the only thing bothering Aaron. Had David been hanging out with Peter just the day before his death? Had they been in Blackhawk or in Bern? Why had no one seen the car that had taken David's life? Why had David been carrying a book by that asshole and nothing else?

As Aaron hung up the phone, the best way to find out what had been going on occurred to him. He would drive to Bern and finally, once and for all, have it out with Peter Toombs. He threw a case of beer on the passenger side floor of his pick-up and stuffed his rifle behind the seat. Maybe they'd have a couple beers and get this out of the way, Aaron thought. And if not, well, only he knew about the rifle.

***

Three men were about to converge on Peter Toombs. His friend, Connor Parrish, flying in from the west, hoping to find the man he knew in good health. Aaron Doyle, coming from the northeast, ready for a confrontation but secretly hoping to connect with the only other man who'd been intimate with his now-deceased wife. From the southeast, Sergeant Raines, Blackhawk P.D., a short list of questions in his pocket, a longer list in his head, both for Peter Toombs whom he suspected of knowing more about David Ward's sudden death than he let on. Of the three, Peter expected Raines, longed for Connor, and would wait for Aaron. He would get all three of them closer than he expected.

There was only one road into Bern. It was amazing that these three men did not pass each other on the way. None of the three stopped to wonder if they'd leave Bern alive. If they had, perhaps they would have turned around and gone home, leaving Peter Toombs alone to whatever fate God and Bern had planned for him. Perhaps they each would have continued on, curiosity or concern getting the better of them. As it was, all three men—Connor Parrish, Sergeant Raines and Aaron Doyle—arrived in Bern before dusk. Before the owls could begin crying down the dark.

CHAPTER

~26~

Sergeant Raines did not think that Peter Toombs ran over David Ward and left the scene. From what he could gather, David had been Peter's only friend after the break-up between Peter and Diana. Mark and Pam Ward regaled Raines with the story of Diana's funeral, her previous miscarriage and quite a number of unpleasant things concerning Peter Toombs. Did that make him a hit-and-run murderer? No, it did not.

What Raines wanted to know was whether or not Peter had been with David anytime in the last few days. He wanted to know if and when Peter had signed the book David had had with him at the time of the accident. The book, a brand-new copy of *Takes My Life*, was nestled in Raines's briefcase along with a few standard witness statement forms and a tape recorder.

Raines had been tempted to read the book. If he'd still been in the Major Crimes division in Salt Lake City, he could have charged a copy to the department and called it research. Instead of reading the book, he had settled for a plot synopsis from Mrs. Raines, a high school English teacher who had had both Peter Toombs and David Ward in the same class and later Diana Ward. She claimed to have always tried to steer Peter away from "all that horror nonsense" as she put it. Still, she bought both of his books and many of the magazines his short fiction had appeared in. She would not, however, watch *Graveyard Paradise*. Satisfied with the rundown from his wife, Raines did not read any of Peter's work, but it was there if he changed his mind.

Raines did not consider audio books to be reading. He'd been able to check out the taped version of *Scream Queen* from the Blackhawk Public Library. The tapes of *Takes My Life* were out and not due for another week. Peter himself performed both audio versions, as per Peter's contracts. Raines recognized the voice as the one he'd heard on the phone. It was a voice that was both scared and scary at the same time. Raines did not care for the voice. It sounded too much like some of the crazies he'd interviewed over the years. It was the voice of a man who could snap at any time, with zero warning.

Mrs. Raines had previously listened to these tapes and told her husband to skip ahead to the third tape out of four. Sergeant Raines, a man used to listening to his wife's advice, did so. For a man also used to crime scenes of varying levels of gore, the snippet of story that curled itself into his head worried him more than the man's voice alone had done.

Raines let Peter's voice fill his head:

Chapter Three.

J.D. recognized the knife for what it was when Alice put it in his hand. He couldn't bring himself to look at it but it felt huge. Like one of those jungle-hacking machetes in an adventure movie about lost Mayan gold. He wanted to deny what was happening, shrug it off as some bad dream. After what he and Alice had done in the Forest, this must be the ultimate wet dream gone wrong.

Alice took his other hand and led him from the kitchen into the living room. Her dad was sitting in his recliner, a newspaper preventing him from seeing J.D.'s reflection in the TV set. J.D. wasn't even sure he believed the story Alice had told him of the bad things her father had done to her. She wouldn't come right out and say it but J.D. knew what she had meant. Abuse. Rape. Incest. To J.D., who only an hour before had lost his virginity to this girl Alice, those concepts were still TV-movie ideas. Alice spoke as one intimately aware of those horrors. So how could he not do what Alice wanted him to do?

Slowly, J.D. raised the knife, really seeing its length for the first time. Alice was right there, whispering in his ear. "Just like I did with that skank Stacy. The first one is the hardest. After that, the knife does most of the work itself."

Alice was wrong about that. J.D.'s arm hurt so bad that he hardly noticed all the blood Alice's dad had sprayed on him.

Writing about kids killing their parents (or their friends' parents) did not seem like wholesome entertainment to Raines. In fact, it seemed like a colossal waste of time and talent to him. He understood how his wife felt about having a student go on to be successful with some of the tools she believed she had taught him. However this situation turned out, he would put his foot down about what kind of "literature" Mrs. Raines could bring into their home.

While his opinion of Peter Toombs's character had suffered a major blow in the eyes of Sergeant Raines, it still did not make him a killer. And after establishing Peter's whereabouts for the last few days and a few questions to the man himself, Sergeant Raines hoped his business with the author would be done. If he could not establish a convincing alibi for the time leading up to the death of David Ward, well, Raines would deal with that when he had to.

He left Blackhawk just before two o'clock. Barring any traffic—this being a weekday, he did not expect any—Raines could be in Bern within the hour. He told his wife that he should be back for a late supper. It was not like Raines to lie to his wife and this wasn't really a lie. He didn't know.

***

Raines was seven cars back from the accident that delayed his arrival in Bern. He could have gotten out of his car and helped out. He could have used the radio in his unmarked car to check out the situation. He could have flipped on his own lights and sirens and made his way through the pile up. He did none of these things. Instead, he rolled down his window and let the canyon breeze blow through the car. He had turned off the tapes of Peter Toombs describing an uncouth father-daughter relationship and various acts of teen sex and murder. He sat there wondering what kind of person could write such things (it had not occurred to him to further question what kind of person reads that kind of trash, as it would implicate his wife as a deviant), and be happy with themselves.

Adding this to what he'd been told about Peter Toombs, Raines assumed that maybe the writer wasn't so happy. Even his wife had mentioned that, as a teen, Peter had seemed dark and moody. And it wasn't just the black fingernail polish and eyeliner that he wore, she said. "He wrote a poem once," Mrs. Raines told her husband. "It was about how this guy killed himself and left a note for his girlfriend. When she finished the note, she used his gun to commit suicide, too. Very Romeo and Juliet, don't you think?"

Raines didn't think that at all. If this guy went nuts at his dead ex-girlfriend's funeral—going into a rage before the service, according to the woman's parents—what else was he apt to do? Raines reminded himself that none of this made Peter a murderer. It did, however, make Peter a potentially dangerous subject. Sitting in his car, waiting for the traffic to clear, Sergeant Raines checked the clips of his police-issue Glock 19. A woman sitting in the passenger seat of a car next to him saw this and scrunched tighter against the male driver. Raines smiled then turned the stereo on. He always had it set to sports radio and hearing the day's baseball scores helped him focus on the task at hand.

The Dodgers and Giants were set to play a three game series starting that night at Dodger Stadium. Raines liked the San Diego Padres and wished that both the Dodgers and Giants could lose. By the time he reached Peter's home in Bern, the game had begun.

CHAPTER

~27~

If Aaron had been able to go the speeds he'd wanted, he most certainly would have passed the more conservative Sergeant Raines. As it was, the traffic had not cleared before he entered the canyon and slow was the order of the day. If he didn't believe that Peter knew something about what had happened to David, he would not be on this road. Since her death, Aaron had only visited Diana's grave twice: once when the headstone was ready to be placed and again on their anniversary. Yes, he loved her and missed her, but the few days he'd spent in Bern were enough to creep him out. He had stayed in town for a few days after the ceremony just to try it out. Some old guy in the bookstore looked at him funny when he went to find a book on the history of the town. A girl—a really old girl—with blond pigtails hit on him in the diner. And, before he left, some lawyer guy asked him how long he planned on being in town and how often he planned on visiting. Using a day to go back there now was not Aaron's idea of a well-spent day. Good thing he remembered the beer.

But this goddamn traffic was pissing him off. He couldn't have a drink because if there were an accident he would be busted. Too many cops directing traffic. He knew right where they could direct it.

He loved Diana with all his heart but there were still

things that bugged him. He didn't mean to hit her that one day. But why did she have to make a tape for Peter? Why did Peter have to be such a smug bastard, asking Aaron for permission to contact his wife? Diana married Aaron Doyle, not Peter Toombs. If Aaron had to rub that fact in like salting a wound, then he would. But Diana had not cried out for Aaron when she had her first seizure. Then again, she hadn't called for Peter either. She had cried out for her baby.

Baby? That was the first Aaron had heard of any baby. To begin with, he'd thought that she was pregnant and had not yet told him. He dropped that idea when he heard a boy's name in between the wails. "Kurt," she had cried. "Don't hurt my baby, my little Kurt." A few tests while Diana was unconscious completely ended any idea that she might have been pregnant at that time.

So well before the medical history interview and the time that Diana had finally told Aaron that she had miscarried Peter's child, Aaron knew. He asked her parents and they confirmed it. They asked him not to mention it to her, especially not now, when Death was knocking at her door. Diana told him the whole story once they arrived home, after the interview. That, really, was the night Aaron started drinking.

He hit her because he knew she was dying. He was the one who had to watch her deteriorate. He was the one trying to keep the bills and the insurance claims straight. He was the one answering questions when her friends called. He was the one who had to tell them she was having a good day, even if they could her Diana screaming in the background.

He was the one who was there for her, not Peter Toombs. As much as he knew Diana loved him, he also knew that she still had feelings for Peter. When he heard her say it, cementing his greatest fear, he lost it. He waited to confront her about it until after she'd finished her damnable recording. And it was just once; one slap across the face of a dying woman.

He wasn't such a bad guy, he told himself. He wanted desperately to believe it. If Peter Toombs was the only person he had to convince, he would do so.

He would, if this damn traffic would MOVE! Looking around, checking the perimeter for cops, Aaron pulled a can of beer from the pack and opened it. Since he wasn't going anywhere, he leaned down and took a sip from the can. And then another. And another. By the time he made his way around the wreck, he had drunk six beers and was close to being wrecked himself. He barely noticed that he was listening to the pre-game show of that night's Dodgers-Giants contest. If he had, he would have turned it off. Aaron did not care for baseball.

CHAPTER
~28~

While Sergeant Raines and Aaron Doyle were on the canyon road into Bern, Connor Parrish was waiting in line for his rental car. It had been a pleasant trip, so far. He was momentarily mobbed in LAX and he signed some autographs. On the plane, three people recognized him but only two were fans. The other was a middle-aged woman who requested a seat change after discovering she was assigned the seat next to Connor. In a strange way, that was more flattering than the autograph hounds. Once the plane landed in Salt Lake City, however, it was a whole new ballgame. Not one single person came up to him, asking for an autograph. No one even whispered that they thought, maybe, he might be... no, he couldn't be. In this case he was.

This was his first visit to Salt Lake, and Utah as a whole. The sight of so many young men in tailored suits waiting at the gates startled him. They all seemed to be members of some club, each with their little nametags pinned to the suits. If things became jovial, he would ask Peter about them.

The line at the rental car counter took longer than boarding and exiting the plane combined had taken. He remembered reading somewhere that Salt Lake City had almost no taxi service. If you didn't have a car, you took the bus or the new train that ran through the city. If he'd planned on staying in the city, it would not have been a problem. As it was, he had about 75 miles to drive before reaching his friend. He could have called Peter for a ride but that would have ruined the surprise. Also, whatever it was that was bothering Peter, Connor wanted to see it. If it was something that Peter could hide, he had less chance of discarding any evidence if he was unprepared for Connor's arrival. Connor, on the other hand, was well prepared. He had a map to Bern and directions to Peter's house. He had Alcoholics Anonymous and Narcotics Anonymous pamphlets. He even had a Sex Addicts Anonymous leaflet, just in case. He had thought of the range of problems that Peter might be facing and briefly thought of his agent telling him to get one of those phones that could tell him when to turn. Connor knew about Diana, the lost love Peter told him about one night over a few beers. Peter had still been drinking Heineken at the time. Depression, suicide, grief, drugs, alcohol, and sex: these were problems Connor could help Peter get through. If only he could get through the rental car line.

Connor did not yet know about the traffic jam on the road to Bern, but he would find out soon enough. He just hoped to get into the car in time to find a radio station playing the Dodgers versus the Giants game. He hated to miss the first pitch. Being a Hollywood guy, the Dodgers were his team.

CHAPTER

~29~

The accident impeding the highway was not as much of an accident as it would seem. It was meant to stall people from getting into or out of Bern. In the cases of Aaron, Connor, and Raines, it was doing its job. A southwest bound freezer truck had jack-knifed then turned over, blocking the last passing zone before the road became a two-lane jaunt straight into Bern. If it seemed almost too well placed, it was. Both directions became one lane sooner than usual and that caused the back up. Cars could get around to either side of the overturned trailer, but the Utah Highway Patrol were searching vehicles to see if anyone had possibly seen or picked up the driver of the truck. The road had been clear before the accident, with the closest vehicle a good two miles away at the time.

Except, that was, for the getaway car used by Chuck and Nicholas Weiss to get back to Bern after turning the truck. It was not an easy thing to do. Chuck, who drove the truck to its appointed destination, had to hit the brakes at just the right time to cause the jack-knife. Once that happened, he had to pray that the truck would turn driver's side up. He knew the Lerners would take care of his family if something went wrong, but he did not want his little brother Nick (Chuck was thirty-eight and Nick thirty-four) to see him go up in a fireball.

Everything went right. Chuck and Nick burned rubber out of there and didn't see another car for five miles on their side of the crash. It wasn't a permanent solution. It was only meant to give the citizens of Bern a few precious hours to conduct some unsavory business. Such business was best conducted without outside interruption.

The beat-up, yellow Toyota Chuck and Nick sped away in did not have a stereo. They had no idea there was a game going on besides the one being played by the Bern townspeople. And, frankly, they did not care at all.

UHP and their tow trucks managed to get the tractor-trailer upright and towed away around five o'clock. No injuries but the missing driver certainly bothered them. The truck had been reported stolen that morning but there were no witnesses to the theft. Strange, true, but no one was hurt. The trailer was empty and even the truck was not as badly damaged as it could have been. The consensus was that fingerprints would turn up something and they'd pursue it after that. Until then, the road was finally clear and people could get on with their business whatever their business might be. None of them listened to the game, either.

CHAPTER

~30~

Peter did not know about the overturned trailer. He didn't know there was a game on tonight. He didn't know that he was about to be visited by three men, one he was familiar with, one he was acquainted with, and one mostly a stranger. If he had known these things, he might have put them in Dickensian terms. He knew his past well; he had a passing acquaintance with the present; and he knew very little about the future. He felt something was coming, though. In the subtext of Diana's tape to him, there was a warning about the future. If it was a warning not to come to Bern, he wished he had heard it three months ago. If it was a warning not to love her as much as he did, he would never hear it.

He had taken the cassette out of the player and held it in his hands for over an hour. More than once during that hour Peter came close to breaking the cassette in two and spilling its guts into his lap. Twice he pulled his arm back, ready to hurl to tape at the wall just to see it shatter into a million pieces. He did neither of these things because they reminded him how easy it was to take a life (Diana, Ben, David, Kurt), and how horrible it was to watch someone die. He had only witnessed Ben's death firsthand and he thought that he got off easy. Ben had died quickly and with no forethought of it happening. Diana had a year to prepare for her end but the last few hours must have been horrible. David, he still didn't know exactly what had happened to David. Maybe he went fast, too. And Kurt... Kurt didn't even get a fair shake at it.

Peter, who had written death and dying and many things beyond, was sick and tired of it. He wanted life, finally, and he wanted it on his terms. No one in this shitty tourist-trap town was going to stop him from living the life he wanted to live. No one was going to hold him back from being a whole person. That included Diana. Sadly, that had to include Kurt, as well.

He left the things he'd packed sitting where they were and walked out his front door. He had no plan except to face whatever was waiting for him in the cemetery. Luckily for him, the cavalry would be arriving shortly.

***

They knew he would come. They knew since the moment he arrived in town. They knew he was the one. All the work up to this time would be fulfilled. They had to tell him to stay out so that he would want nothing more than he wanted in. And when he came, he would be welcomed. He belonged here. They all knew. His place was reserved for him, his place at the table set. They did not want to hurt any of their own, but they all knew that sacrifice was rule number one. When your time came, you could go with dignity or spurned. Every citizen decided their own outcome. Those like the bookseller who chose not to cooperate went harshly and without proper preparation. Those like the woman were given time to ready themselves. Those like the watcher, who performed their tasks unto their end, were given special honors when their time came. None knew when their time would be but all were ready to sacrifice of themselves. He would be, too. It had been only a matter of time. Now, time was near its end. And he would come to them.

The Judge, the Lawyer, the Cook, and the Whore waited for him; the Writer. The Watcher and the Bookseller waited, but with less enthusiasm. Their ends had come and they could no longer affect the goings-on. The Woman, also known as the Lover and the Childless Mother, waited for the Writer as well. Yes, her end had come, but she still had a part to play before the Writer could truly become one of them.

Unfortunately, this twisted band of Tarot card rejects did not expect the three cards yet to come: The Bailiff, the Man Who Played Death, and the Drunk, also known as the Jilted Lover. They would come, too, but for much different reasons. The Town was always happy to have more, as long as none planned to leave. None could be sure if any of the newcomers would leave. Many try to escape. But if one were to ask the Woman, she could testify to the fact that leaving did not mean you had truly escaped.

They waited. It would not be long now. Once his anger was riled again, he would come. The celebration would begin in earnest. Lovers would be reunited. Some would meet their end and some would find new beginnings. It was all a grand, vicious cycle. A wheel of life covered in razor blades and salt. Oh what merriment would be had by all! Oh what suffering to be shared!

Peter, of course, knew none of this as he ran out of his house and into the waiting arms of a town that had gone berserk. Even if he did know, he probably would have run just as fast to get there. Suffering, after all, was second nature to him. Hell, he might even have run faster.

The giant in his chest was loose again and it would not stop until it had finally caught up with him.

CHAPTER
~31~

Someone had an oldies station playing. Peter couldn't tell where, exactly, the music was coming from. For all he knew, it was coming from his own head. The first song he recognized was Harry Nilsson singing "Without You."

Put a stake in me, he thought. *I must be done.* He laughed at the joke, knowing only Diana would get it. Even as he ran towards whatever awaited him in the Bern cemetery, he still found a moment to laugh. "Without You" was the type of song he'd pick to play for Diana, noting the irony of it being used in a horror movie. If he had time to think, Peter might have thought it more appropriate for the town to play "Everyone's Talking."

The music faded and changed to a baseball game. The Giants and Dodgers were in the seventh inning. The Giants lead stood at four to two. Peter didn't hear who was batting before the phantom radio clicked off.

Down two runs in the seventh, he thought. *I can do this. Let's rock. Bring in the set-up man and I'll close it down in the ninth. Strike out the side and go home.*

He slowed down as he reached the cemetery gates. A bonfire raged near where he knew Diana's grave to be. Shadow bodies surrounded the fire, circling the flames. Some held their arms up to the sky and others had their arms straight out in front of them. Peter couldn't see any faces but saw bouncing pigtails that could only belong to Helga. Also, he couldn't recall seeing anyone else in town as tall as Judge Lerner. So far, it looked like none of them had seen him, either.

After walking a yard beyond the gates, Peter felt a hand clamp down on his shoulder. He didn't scream but it was close. He wanted to turn around but the hand held firm.

"Don't move, Peter. It's Connor. What the hell is going on in there?"

"I don't know," Peter answered after hearing his friend's voice. "Whatever it is, I'm supposed to be there. Listen…"

Both men stood still, ears waiting for any sound that might come. Connor could only hear the fire and the mumbled chanting of the congregation.

"You don't hear it, do you? You don't hear them calling my name. Listen, it's there. I have to go in and face the giant before he tears my heart out and I lose Diana forever."

Connor shook Peter. This wasn't exactly the reunion he had expected. "Diana is dead, Peter. I know that is hard for you to accept. But she's dead. You saw her buried. You told me you saw her body."

"I don't think that matters. Somehow I think she is coming back or she's already here. And if she is, she's going to be with them. I have to save her from them."

"Save who from what them?" another voice said from behind Connor and Peter.

"Shit," Peter said. "Aaron, hi, how are you?" Connor's hand fell from Peter as Peter stood to face Aaron.

"Cut it out, Toombs. Tell me what the hell is going on here?"

"I don't think he really knows," Connor said.

Aaron reached for Connor but stumbled. Connor put his hands out and braced him. The smell of Keystone Light beer wafted from Aaron, nearly overcoming the smell of the bonfire. Connor held him like that until he was able to straighten himself out.

"Sorry," Aaron said. "I had a little to drink on the way up here. Hell, I don't even know why I'm here. No, that's not right. I came up here 'cause you killed David." Aaron lunged for Peter. He slipped on a patch of wet grass and came within three inches of cracking his skull on a headstone. His body relaxed and his arms sprawled out. Before Connor or Peter could check to see if Aaron had hurt himself, he was snoring.

"Friend of yours?" Connor asked.

"Not really. This is... was Diana's husband. I guess he thinks I killed her brother, too."

"Did you?"

"No, but some cop called and wants to talk to me."

"You mean that cop?"

Peter turned to the gate where Connor was pointing. He could make out the shape of a man holding a gun.

"Yeah, most likely, that's Sergeant Raines."

"Do you want to say hello?"

"No. Let's see where he goes."

***

The first car Raines saw when he arrived in Bern belonged to Aaron Doyle. He knew because his crime lab had checked it against the tire tracks found at the scene of David Ward's death. Like most police officers, Raines did not believe in coincidence. Either Doyle was here to confront Peter Toombs or the two of them were mired in some conspiracy. After talking to both men, the first option seemed more likely.

A car parked just in front of Doyle's had rental car stickers on it. Bern was, after all, a tourist town. Raines made a mental note of it then filed it away.

He tried to ignore the absence of people, but the stillness almost overwhelmed him. No one window shopping along Bern's main street. No lights on in the stores even though it was nearly dark. As he walked farther into town, a warning bell went off in his head.

Fire. He smelled fire.

Following the scent like one of the K-9 units, he soon saw the flames that were the source of the smoke. He ran in the direction of the flames, pulling a cell phone from one pocket as he did so.

At the cemetery entrance, he saw a clearer picture of the flames. It didn't strike him as odd that the citizens of a town would gather together around a bonfire. He did question the legality of having such an event inside a graveyard. Then he heard voices that sounded like arguing, hidden among the headstones. He turned to better hear the voices but they were soon overwhelmed by voices from the bonfire. And the screaming of a woman.

CHAPTER

~32~

Peter and Connor were watching Raines when they heard the scream. They saw him put what they thought was a gun but was a cell phone, back into his pocket before running towards the fire.

Peter wanted to run, too. He knew that scream, although it was louder and filled with more pain than he ever remembered it being. He knew that if Aaron was conscious, he would recognize the sound as well.

The screaming woman was Diana. How that could be, Peter did not know. He began to walk around fallen headstones getting closer to the fire and the Bern-folk.

"Wait, Peter," Connor yelled. "You can't go over there. They all look nuts."

"I have to," he said. "I'm a part of this. I have to know what happened to Diana. I have to face the giant." Peter walked away without hearing another word from Connor.

Connor, who had scared a nation through film, felt a trickle of wetness at his crotch. *Wet kill*, he thought. *They wet killed me like I was a high school girl in a spook alley.*

He followed his friend.

***

Raines didn't see the two men come up behind him. If he had, they both could have been shot. His entire focus was on the fire, the people surrounding it, and the woman who seemed to be at the center of the group. She was being passed around, person to person, ash mixing with the dirt on her once white garment. As he came closer, he saw that she was wearing a wedding gown.

She continued screaming as she was handed from body to body. Some groped her, some kissed her; she kept screaming.

Raines pulled his gun and checked that it was loaded. It always was but he needed to be sure. Despite the fear tightening his gut and his genitals, it was time to be a cop.

"All you fucking weirdoes freeze," he yelled, trying to point the gun at all of them. "Let the woman go!"

Judge Lerner, draped in a black velvet robe in mockery of the one he wore on the bench, removed himself from the mass of writhing bodies.

"Officer, so good of you to join us. Please, put down the weapon and no will get hurt."

"You stay right where you are, freak," Raines said, now pointing the gun directly at Judge Lerner.

Ignoring the gun, the judge looked over Raines's shoulder, noticing Peter and Connor for the first time.

"I didn't know you had back-up," he said.

Raines turned around, seeing the other men for a brief moment before being swarmed by members of the mob. Peter tried to rush forward and help but Connor held him back. Three shots were fired but with all the screaming, Peter couldn't tell if they hit anyone. When the swarm cleared, only the body of Sergeant Raines remained on the ground.

His head was now in the hands of Judge Lerner.

"You see, Mr. Toombs," Judge Lerner intoned. "Everyone who aids in your cause dies. You never should have come here. As trite as it sounds, we can never let you leave."

"I just want to see Diana. She's her, isn't she? Please, let me see her."

"She is here and I believe she wants to see you, too."

"No, Peter," Connor interrupted. "Don't listen. This fucker is trying to pull some Christopher Lee voodoo bullshit on you. Don't listen. Diana is dead."

"But you heard her screaming, didn't you?" Peter asked. "She needs me."

"Don't do it, Peter. They are just going to show you some woman to make you think it is Diana and then kill all of us. You, me, and…" Connor stopped, remembering the unconscious Aaron Doyle, left out of this madness.

"And who?" Judge Lerner asked. "Who else have you brought here?"

"And Raines, the cop. But you already killed him."

"No, we didn't. You did." Lerner threw the severed head at Connor who caught it out of pure reflex but held on to show he wasn't as afraid as he felt. Blood seeping from the exposed neck dribbled onto Connor but he held tight to the head. *It's just a movie prop*, he thought. *You've held dozens of them, been drenched in more blood than this. Think of it as fake and you'll be fine.*

But it isn't fake. All those years of Karo syrup and red food coloring didn't prepare Connor for real blood. He was holding a recently decapitated head and it was still bleeding on him. He dropped the head which bounced off his right foot, sounding vaguely like dropping a rotten grapefruit. He bent over and began heaving.

I'm never going to eat grapefruit again, he thought.

Which he knew to be true, one way or another.

Peter missed getting sprayed with both blood and vomit only because he was jumping up and down, trying to see where the crowd had taken the woman he thought to be

Diana. Much of the screaming had been replaced with laughter at Connor's expense. If Connor could keep the judge busy and the Bern citizens distracted, Peter might be able to find the love of his life.

Whoever had been playing oldies started again. This time, Peter was more certain that the music came from his own head. No one at that moment would play "Last Kiss" by J. Frank Wilson and the Cavaliers. *No one who doesn't want to keep taunting me*, Peter thought. *Give me Metallica or give me death.*

A small group had separated from the main body of the crowd. Peter could see the younger Lerner leading them. The Judge was still occupied with laughing at Connor. Peter broke away and managed to pick up the splinter group's trail.

In following them, he passed Diana's grave. The marker was toppled over and a hole was in the ground where the grass had not yet finished growing. He didn't know for sure but it looked more like someone had clawed their way out from below than being dug out.

The hole, except for broken pieces of an expensive casket and a few shards of yellowed fabric, was empty.

Peter pulled himself away from the violated earth before he fell in. The mini-mob was still in sight. He wasn't sure why, but he knew that Diana must be with them. The fact of her death was cloudier than ever.

CHAPTER

~33~

Aaron Doyle was having a nightmare. He was drunk and found himself in a cemetery with a man he hated and someone who talked just like a movie monster. There was a fire somewhere and a lot of people screaming. He could hear people trying to talk to him, or talking about him, but none of it filtered through the screams.

One scream in particular worried him. It sounded just like Diana had sounded at the worst heights of her pain. The days when the medication couldn't cut through the concrete wall of physical torture. The times when Diana's brain rebelled against her, creating a frothy-mouthed she-demon intent on hurting as many people as possible, just so they could feel a tenth of what she felt.

Those were the bad days. And in this nightmare, that is all Aaron could remember. It was strange, after so long with Diana's claims of living in Hell, the quiet of the house after her passing was worse. Something, even pain, was better than nothing.

And he hated Peter Toombs even more for thinking he knew what her pain was.

Toombs was here in the nightmare now but fading, following the fire, I hope he falls in, Aaron's dream-self told him. I hope he burns.

He felt a familiar tickle and knew he had to wake up before he pissed his pants. He stretched out his arms, waking up. His hands touched the cold granite of tombstones and he remembered it wasn't a nightmare after all.

CHAPTER
~34~

Diana. Diana. Diana.

They kept calling her that. People she knew from somewhere or thought she should know. They all called her Diana.

That must be her name, then. If so many people called her that, then it must be her name. She couldn't remember.

Some of the crowd around her parted, still chanting her name, and she could see a face she was positive she knew. Peter.

Peter running toward her, through the bonfire.

Peter, calling her Diana, like everyone else had.

Despite the fire, everything seemed dark to her. She started to cry and her vision doubled. She hoped someone would be there to catch her when she fainted.

Peter ran toward the woman, pushing aside those villagers who did not move on their own. He saw the judge smile for a moment just before the woman's knees buckled and gravity took over. He tripped over a low headstone and stretched his arms out. He got his hands under her but the weight of her slack body and Peter's momentum brought them to ground. Peter's arms were the first to hit the granite slab of an upraised headstone.

None of the cloaked bodies surrounding him moved when they heard Peter's arms break or when he screamed. The woman whose body concealed the compound fractures of Peter's forearms didn't stir from her faint. Her hair swooshed up and covered her eyes.

Peter also lay still, his stomach and legs on the wet ground of the cemetery, his shattered arms caught between a cold headstone and the warm body he tried to catch. He tried to save her from falling and now couldn't even move to pick her up and carry her away from these maniacs.

He lifted his head as far as he could and felt a twinge of recognition that hurt worse than the pain shooting from his arms into his head.

He knew her, yes.

She wasn't Diana. Peter screamed again, unsure when he would ever stop.

**

Connor knew he should continue to follow this splinter group but when he heard Peter scream and scream again, he turned around and sprinted toward the screaming.

He saw a prostrate body hugging a headstone and weeping.

"Aaron, get up," he said. "Peter needs us and so does that woman."

"It's her, isn't?" Aaron said. "It's Diana and they are going to kill her again."

"Peter won't let them and we have to help. Now get up, get your shit together, and let's go."

Aaron stood up, shook the graveyard dust off himself and took a deep breath.

"OK," Aaron said. "Let's go."

**

"Do you see, Mr. Toombs?" Judge Lerner said, now standing over Peter and the woman who hid his broken arms. He placed a foot on Peter's ass, applying enough pressure to take Peter's screams up another notch. "Do you see? Diana is dead but we brought her back. She has much power and we were all disappointed that she died so young and before we could harness her potential. So we had to bring her back the best that we could. Of course, none of us have the power to raise the dead, as you so often do in your tales. We found the next best thing."

Lerner snapped his fingers and three of the villagers appeared to lift the woman off of Peter's arms, relieving some of his physical pain. He sucked in air and dust, just enough to ask one question.

"Why Debbie?"

"Next best thing, Mr. Toombs," Lerner said. He kicked Peter in the shoulder. Peter screamed again and didn't stop until he was out of breath. He wanted to scream more but couldn't muster the lung power. His arms were stretched out before him, bent the wrong way over the low headstone. Both arms seemed to have grown extra elbows somewhere between his wrists and his natural elbows. There was blood, he could feel it but it wasn't gushing, just puddling around the shards of stark white bone protruding from the soft skin of his forearms. The blood pooled in the shallow shadow of the headstone, making the grass around it that much blacker.

The mob shuffled away, Lerner in the lead followed by the three villagers carrying Debbie.

For a moment, Peter was alone with his pain.

CHAPTER
~35~

For a moment, Peter was alone. Diana was still dead. David was still dead. Debbie, at least, had been found, although whether she would survive the night was still under question. Raines still had his head cut off and Peter had no idea what happened to Aaron and Connor. Maybe they were dead, too.

Peter was alone, for a moment.

***

The vibrations from his arms turned into music in his head. Something with too much reverb and the knob cranked to eleven. Thunder blasts from the bass and drums beat against his skull. At first, he thought this would be one of those long instrumentals, some prog-rock bullshit that could go on for hours and didn't make a lick of sense.

A missed chord flared through his left arm and he opened his eyes. He tried to bring his hands to his face to rub his eyes, to wake up, to be rid of the nightmare and couldn't. He couldn't feel his hands but white fire filled the rest of his flesh up to his shoulders.

"Don't move, Peter," Connor said from somewhere Peter couldn't see. "Your arms are broken and if you move any more, it's going to hurt like hell.'

"Christ, are those bones poking through?" Aaron asked, pointing at sharp flecks of granite sticking to Peter's arms. Connor held back from slapping him, knowing that would only make things worse. They needed to cooperate.

"It's not Diana," Peter said, coughing as he did. "She's not Diana."

"What the fuck do you mean?" Aaron said, feeling the hate for Peter rise again.

"Who is it, Peter?" Connor asked, ready to hold Aaron back if needed.

"It's Debbie. We have to save her. They'll kill her," Peter said. He closed his eyes and let the music, too much reverb and all, take him over. For a moment, he was alone again.

"This is all his fault," Aaron said. "I should just break his arms off the rest of the way and beat him to death with his own hands."

Connor did slap him for saying that. "Listen you little shit. We have to pick him up—gently—and go after that mob. He says they are going to kill that woman, Diana, Debbie, whoever the fuck she is. She's in danger. He tried to save her while you were catnapping and now he has two busted arms for it and is probably going crazy."

"Fuck him. Where's that cop?"

Connor grabbed Aaron by the ears and brought their faces close enough for their noses to touch.

"You see this blood? It isn't mine, motherfucker."

Aaron gagged but couldn't hold it back. What little remained in his stomach now mixed with the blood on Connor's face. Connor didn't let go of Aaron's ears right away. Instead, he used them to force Connor's face toward the ground but away from Peter. He wanted to punch him, to take him out of the picture and finish this alone. He wasn't strong enough to lift Peter without causing him more harm, so he still needed Aaron.

"If you are done vomiting," Connor said, "I'll let you go and we can get on with this."

"I'm done." Aaron wiped his mouth with one arm and his brow with the other. "Let's get those bastards."

Connor released Aaron's ears and let him stand back up. He motioned for Aaron to get on one side of Peter as he went to the other.

"We need to be careful. We don't want to hurt him any more than he already is."

"We he says. Speak for yourself, pal."

"Yes, we. He's the only one who might have a clue where those freaks are going."

"Bullshit," Aaron said and pointed toward the house on the hill. A jagged line of torches marched toward the front door.

"Just shut up and help me. And quit being an asshole, if you can."

"Do my best."

***

The record in Peter's head began to skip. It got louder, then almost disappeared only to come back at full strength. He still hadn't pinpointed the source, which wild group of cheap rock stars was running a sound check within the walls of his skull.

Then came the sensation of being lifted, as if he were going to crowd surf. As far as he knew his hands remained on the ground, connected to the rest of him by thin threads of solid pain. Who needs hands anyway, he thought. Certainly not a writer.

Definitely not me. They'll never let me write again. I'll be stuck here, none of my mail will go out and they'll never let me go. Just kill me. This crowd should just drop me where

I am and let me rot.

"Drop me," Peter said. "Lemme go. Never get out. Gotta leave. Drop me."

"Peter, it's Connor. I've got you. Me and Aaron have you. We're gonna save Diana."

"It's not Diana," Peter said, his voice regaining some strength. "It's Debbie, Diana's sister. They took her when they killed David, I think. And they aren't going to let her go."

"Then we'll take her," Aaron said. "We'll take her back and fuck them up when we do."

"Put me down, guys," Peter said. "You can't carry me all the way."

Peter winced at the pain in his arms and seeing just how broken they were almost made him pass out again. He breathed deep and steadied himself. "Give me your shirts. I need to sling my arms."

Connor took off his shirt and tied it around Peter's neck. He kicked Aaron in the shin and soon the second sling was tied and ready.

"One of you will have to move my arms into the slings. I can't do it."

"Fuck off," Aaron said. "I'm not touching you."

Connor scowled at Aaron before nodding at Peter.

"Just be careful, please," Peter said to his friend.

"I'll go slow," Connor said. "Tell me if you need me to stop."

"Just listen for the scream," Peter said, then paused. "OK, I'm ready."

CHAPTER

~36~

The younger Lerner opened the door to Peter's house for his father from the inside. The living room lights were on and someone had the TV on. The villagers carrying Debbie's limp body entered and placed her on the sofa.

"I have everything ready, Dad," Walter Lerner said. "They are all in place, just waiting for Toombs now."

"Good," said the judge. "We do still have his two friends to deal with, as well as placing the police officer's head and body in a more appropriate place."

"Push him in the open grave," a female voice said, from near the TV set.

"Helga, dear, that is exactly what I had in mind," the judge said.

Helga came up to the two men and kissed the elder Lerner as the younger groped her breasts through the ceremonial robe she had on. The judge pushed her away after a few moments.

"More time for this later, once we finish this," he said.

"What are you going to do with her," Helga asked, pointing at Debbie.

"We're going to let her hang around," Walter said, chuckling to himself as he had when he first met Peter.

"And the other one," Helga asked again.

Walter continued to chuckle as his father looked up to the ceiling, smiling like a man who has everything in life he could ever want.

***

Helga sat in front of Debbie, rearranging the unconscious woman's arms. Left folded over right; right over left; one over her breasts, one across her forehead. Debbie's arms, so carefully placed, kept slipping back into her lap.

"You don't take direction very well, do you?" Helga said then stuck her tongue out. Walter Lerner came into the room just before Helga could get the raspberry out of her mouth.

"Dammit, Helga, you'll wake that bitch up." Walter lifted his hand but Helga, still with her tongue out, crawled to him, her long pigtails dragging on the floor.

"You wouldn't hit me," she said. "Not with your dad in the next room."

"Just leave her alone. If she wakes up before we're ready, it'll be your ass."

Helga turned around. "This ass?" she said, shaking her seat at Walter.

"When this is finished, you are going to get it."

"Why do we have to wait?" she said, moving her pert ass closer to Walter.

CHAPTER

~37~

Peter wanted to run. Not a marathon, pace yourself, take it easy because it's a long way kind of run but an all-out, golden sneakers at the Olympics kind of run. The pain in his obliterated arms kept him from reaching the insane speeds he felt he needed to reach. Connor and Aaron tried to match his inconsistent pace while not bumping into Peter but remaining close enough to catch him if he fell.

The house loomed above them, Peter thought. He knew his editor would kick his ass over such a cliché but there was no other word for it. The house looms and trouble awaits.

He stepped in a hole and his body spun, facing the cemetery again. Connor caught him around the waist before he could tumble down the hill and break something else. Aaron reached out to grasp Peter's shoulders and pulled back at the last second.

"Holy shit," Aaron said. "That was close."

"You need to slow down, Peter," Connor said, his arms still around Peter's waist. Peter wanted to shrug off those arms and race to the finish. He had to save Diana.

"I have to save Debbie," Peter said. He twisted around, noting the hole that had caused him to slow down. "I have to save them."

139

"God damn it," Aaron said. "Diana is gone, asshole. I was there. You weren't. Even if she was alive, she wouldn't be yours to save."

"She said she'd come back for me. Essie said so." For a moment, the pain in his heart transcended the pain in his arms. He started to slip out of Connor's arms, ready to give up.

Connor hoisted Peter back to his feet, jostling his arms in the process. Peter screamed, feeling the bones of his arms grate against skin and other pieces of bone.

"Someone still has to save Debbie," Connor said.

"Wipe the dirt out of my eyes, would you?" Peter said

***

The three men continued up the hill toward the childhood home of a woman only two of them knew. Her husband kept his distance, still not trusting the other two. Her first love trudged up the hill, arms and heart broken, determined to fix what he could. The one who never met her walked with his friend, positive he'd be the first to see her on the other side.

Peter avoided all possible holes along the rest of the way, kept his feet if not his head and tried to ignore the waves of torment washing up his arms. They kept a steady pace and reached the house only slightly out of breath. Burnt out torches lay along the walk to the porch. Aaron kicked at one of them, sending it spiraling across the lawn.

"Fucking torches," he said. "Makes you wonder why they left their pitchforks at home."

"They didn't," Peter said. "They are in the house with them, ready to punch a hole through your guts and bleed you out like cattle."

"You first," Aaron said, giving Peter the bird as he did.

CHAPTER

~38~

Blue light spilled through the crack of the open front door. As Peter approached the door, he could hear the faint whirring of the DVD player. He tried to peak through the opening but could only see the TV screen with the DVD logo bouncing from corner to corner.

"Do you see anyone?" Aaron asked. Connor elbowed Aaron, then held a finger to his lips.

Peter stepped back from the door and faced the other two men.

"I didn't see anyone but there are a bunch of dirty footsteps on the floor. They must be upstairs," Peter said.

"Can they see us from the windows," Aaron said.

"If they have someone watching, they would have seen us by now," Connor said.

"Right," said Peter. "You can see the whole cemetery from any of the windows on this side of the house. I spent most of time inside looking at Diana's marker." Peter shuddered, still wondering what Judge Lerner had done with Diana's body and what he and the other townsfolk had planned for Debbie. The shudder sent a jolt of pain from his mangled arms into his head.

"Maybe they did see us and are just hiding, waiting for us to go inside," Aaron said. His own thoughts were muddled from the blow to the head he took. Walking up to the house took more energy than he had thought and now he was not only losing strength but conviction. His wife's body was gone and the people inside this house were the only ones who knew where her body was now. Aaron couldn't hit the man who was trying, desperately, to find out what happened and now to save his sister-in-law. He, really, was the only one of the three men who had any sort of binding relationship with the endangered woman. He clenched his jaw and continued on despite his softening fury. Not seeing any of the townspeople scared him more than if they had been at the door to greet them.

Connor moved forward, careful not to run into Peter's arms. He pushed the door open and had to stop himself from calling out. The footprints became a jumble of mud near the TV, in front of the sofa and again at the foot of the stairs. Still more prints led to the kitchen and out the back door.

"We go up," Peter said as he entered the house with Aaron behind him.

***

Neither Helga nor Walter took a moment to say, "Shouldn't we be watching?" and instead threw themselves onto a recliner, tearing at each other's robes. Debbie, still unconscious, had been locked in the next room and Walter's father was taking care of everything else. All Walter and Helga had left to do was look out the window and watch for Peter.

Aaron saw the fumbling couple first. He kicked Walter in the hip, exposing Walter's genitals to the cool air. Before Walter could say anything, Connor pushed by Aaron and shoved Walter to the ground. Aaron thrust his foot against Helga's stomach and her screams of rage sliced through

Aaron's injured head, forcing him to let her up.

Peter, seeing Helga about to get away, dropped to the floor in front of her, causing her to trip over his body. Her legs caught in her robes and her feet flew up, nearly catching Peter in the face. She landed with her right ear flat on the floor but the rest of her body almost vertical. The contact of her head on the floor muffled the snap of her neck. Her body collapsed, forcing Peter into a prone position, pressing his shattered arms between the floor and his body.

Peter's screams buried Walter's attempts to call for help. Connor hefted him up by the robes, but he squirmed out of them and ran. But Walter could not run toward the body of his dead lover; he ran to the opposite side of the second-story room and right into the room's large window. The window did not break as Walter hoped it might, allowing him some chance to escape. Instead, his head and arms crashed through the glass, slashing the naked flesh of his arms, driving into his eyes, and cutting his throat as Connor and Aaron watched, helpless to stop him.

Peter did not see Walter Lerner's last moments. *Do not lose consciousness*, he repeated to himself. *Stay awake. Finish this.*

CHAPTER
~39~

The Judge heard the screams from the far side of the house. Walter had failed him. Without surprise or worry, Judge Lerner tightened his robes, checked the revolver he held in the belt around his waist, and waited for whoever found him first.

***

"Don't touch me," Peter yelled at Connor as the older man slid Helga's corpse off of the writer. "Find the fucking Judge."

"Come with me," Connor said, grabbing Aaron by the arm. Aaron followed, giving Helga a kick to the ribs.

Peter lay on the floor, catching his breath. His world had gone silent, again, and he waited for something to guide him. He wanted Diana's voice; the gentle tones of the girl he knew in high school, not the frightened and aged voice from the cassette recording. But he knew. Diana was dead. She wasn't coming back for him, or for Aaron, or for her fucking cat that died when she was a girl. He had to come back, though.

He rolled on to his back and with the help of the chair Walter and Helga had been screwing on, managed to stand up. He avoided looking at Helga's body, thinking her pigtails would come to life and wrap around his ankles like snakes. He caught just a brief glimpse of Walter Lerner's moonlit and dead backside, his front side skewered by the window glass. Peter's arms fell to his sides as he stood, banging against his legs. He stifled a scream, not wanting to reveal his upright state to the Judge or anyone else left in the house.

Peter bit the insides of his cheeks and surveyed the room. Two dead, glass and blood littering the floor, pain in his arms, his mouth, his head. He shook his head, feeling the bites inside his mouth and ignoring the pain in his arms. The makeshift slings dangled as limply as his arms, but were not as useless. He sat on the edge of the chair, bent over and found the ends of the slings with his teeth. Peter bit down and tugged. The slings fell away from his body. He used his chin to pull the cloth into his lap. The loose bundle threatened to tumble to the floor and if it did, Peter wouldn't be able to retrieve it. Instead, the cloth stuck to the muck on his pants and held there long enough for Peter to roll it back to his lower abdomen. He pulled his shirt up with his teeth and maneuvered the cloth just high enough to be under the shirt. He let go of the collar, waiting to see if the bundle would stay until taking his next breath. He wiggled so as to get the bottom of his shirt underneath the bulb of material. Satisfied that it would hold, Peter stood, took a long breath, and walked out of the room in search of Judge Lerner and Debbie.

***

Connor and Aaron scoured the second story of the house, checking every closet in every room but did not find any sign of Judge Lerner or Debbie.

"That's it," Aaron said. He started to brush his hair out of his eyes but at the slightest touch to his injured head he drew back his hand. "Everyone is hurt and we have no idea where that kook went."

"Shut up. You'll give us away," Connor said. He would have left Aaron behind, but he felt Peter needed them together. It's like a show; collaboration is key.

They stood in the last room, a small bedroom at the end of hall when the ceiling above them began to creak.

"Is he on the roof" Aaron said. "How the fuck did he get up there?"

"No, wait," Connor said, pushing past Aaron and back into the hall. The retractable attic stairs were down and in front them stood Judge Lerner, holding Debbie is his left arm and a gun in his right hand.

"Let her go," Connor said to the Judge as Aaron caught up to him.

The Judge smiled and fired his revolver at the two men. The bullets struck Connor in chest and stomach. One wayward shot went into the wall, spraying Aaron with plaster and splinters. Connor fell to the floor as the judge emptied his gun at Aaron. One of the three remaining shots grazed Aaron's thigh but the other two missed their marks. Judge Lerner took a step toward Connor then whipped around, dropping Debbie as he did so.

As the judge turned, Peter saw his friend—his only true friend—bleeding out on the floor of his house. The judge pulled the trigger of his gun again, but the gun only clicked against spent shells. Peter expected him to throw the gun, but the judge tucked it back into his robes. He bent to retrieve the still unconscious Debbie. As the judge bent down, Aaron crawled over Connor to grab Connor's murderer.

"Don't," Peter yelled. Both men looked up and stopped their tasks for a moment. Judge Lerner moved first, kicking his leg out behind him and striking Aaron in the face. Aaron slumped back to the floor, his feet inches from the shoes of the dead man behind him.

Peter, arms hanging to his sides, anticipated Judge Lerner's next move. As Lerner reached to move the attic steps back into their slot in the ceiling, Peter kicked out his legs, hitting the support beams of the stairs. The stairs folded up, trapping the judge's arms between the steps. The judge howled and lost his footing. The stairs held him up as he flailed his feet, trying to stand again. One foot struck Debbie and she rolled against the wall. Peter stepped around the stairs and the judge and did his best to move Debbie out of the range of the judge's kicks. He wanted to pick her up and hug her to him, but his arms remained useless. He knelt and checked Debbie's breathing, then did the same for Aaron. Both were still with him.

He shuffled over to Connor, adding a new layer of blood to the canvas of destruction that used to be his pants. He could see there was no need to check for breathing. Connor's eyes and mouth were open in a look of surprise.

"You can't save him. You can't save anyone, you pathetic piece of shit," Judge Lerner said from his pinned position. "You failed everyone. You failed Diana."

"Quiet," Peter said, not caring if the judge heard him or not. "Hush now." Tears began to drop from Peter's face onto Connor's, washing the dust of battle from both of their faces. Peter wanted to reach out and close his friend's eyes, but the pain in his arms prevented it.

Time to end the pain.

CHAPTER

~40~

Peter stood, knowing he would have time to mourn his fallen friend later, and went to the judge. Judge Lerner continued to flail, unable to plant his feet with his arms hung up in the steps of the attic stairs.

"Hush now," Peter told the judge. "It's quiet time."

Peter kicked the stairs, sending bolts of torment through the judge's arms and new screams from his mouth.

"I said hush."

Pushing himself against the stairs, Peter managed to shake the judge free. The judge crumbled against the steps, leaving his face at the level of Peter's stomach. Peter inched toward him, hoisting his shirt up with his teeth. The roll of cloth that had held Peter's broken arms remained caught between his shirt and his pants. He moved so that Judge Lerner's face was in front of the bundle. "Open your mouth," Peter said. He didn't wait for an answer but rather stomped on the judge's foot, opening the judge's mouth for another yelp of pain. As Judge Lerner's mouth opened, Peter pushed the cloth into the judge's mouth, cutting off the scream and the air that kept the judge alive.

Peter batted away the judge's weakened arms as the judge attempted to remove the blockage. Peter knelt and pushed the judge's chin up with his head, further cutting off the oxygen needed for life. Judge Lerner's eyes opened and bulged, the veins filling with blood. The Judge's eyes stood out red as the setting sun against his skin as it turned blue.

"I said hush," Peter repeated as Judge Lerner collapsed against the wall, reaching for the gag. His legs kicked at Peter with less strength in each thrust. His eyes bulged and Peter imagined the words going through the dying man's brain: *You bastard. We never wanted you here. You've killed more than just me.*

A soft kick, an arm slightly raised, and not another gasp from the judge as he slumped down, dead.

Exhausted, Peter lay on his back, surrounded by the dead and the unconscious, and passed into the darkness somewhere between sleep and death.

***

"Peter, wake up."

. . .

"Wake up, Peter."

. . .

"Peter, I need you to wake up."

Diana spoke to him in his retreat from the world. He drifted on a cloud of darkness cried down by the owls outside her house—his house—and wanted nothing more to do with pain and suffering. Diana, as much as he craved a happy life with her from a past well out of reach, knew Diana was pain and suffering. The dark, the dead around him, losing Connor, showed him this. But here again was Diana, calling to him to wake up and face the world.

"Wake up, Mr. Toombs."

That wasn't Diana. It wasn't Connor, not Aaron. The Lerners had been dispatched and Sgt. Raines lay dead in the Bern cemetery. Peter felt a damp cloth on his eyes, wiping away the gum of long sleep from his eyelids. The warmth brought him into the moment and let the light seep in from above. As much as he wished the light to be the final one leading him to beyond, he knew it wasn't.

He opened first his left eye and didn't believe what he saw. It was Diana, leaning over him, telling him to wake up. The sight before him swam and he closed the one eye then opened both to the truth.

"Welcome back, Peter," Debbie said. She held one of Peter's casted hands in hers. His other arm lay heavy at his side, equally ensconced in plaster. The urge to ask where he was passed.

"How did we get here?"

"Sheriffs came up to Bern when no one could reach Sgt. Raines," Debbie said. "They found us all in our old house."

Peter tried to sit up but couldn't find the strength. "Where's Aaron?"

"He's at home. He's fine," Debbie said. "And I'm fine and Connor…"

"Connor's dead, I know."

"Mr. Toombs, please don't fret. You still need to rest," the masculine voice of authority said.

"You must be the doctor," Peter said.

"No, I'm your nurse, Henry. Dr. Udall will be in shortly."

"Thanks."

"She's great," Diana said. "She got Aaron and me out of here in a day."

"How long have I been here?"

"Three days."

CHAPTER

~41~

The red spotlight fell on Peter's face. His gloved hands were folded beneath his chin and, along with the sleeves of his black suit, hid the scars of his many surgeries. His eyes remained closed, allowing the darkness to swirl in his mind. He'd touched the darkness and learned that it was not the friend he'd thought it to be. Behind him, green light splashed on two plaster memorials to fallen friends.

He spoke before lifting his eyes to the camera. "Good evening, gravers. Welcome to Paradise."

He tilted his head and looked right into the camera. "I say paradise but we all know what truly lies here in the graveyard. Our friends and lovers, gone before we were ready. Don't fret; you'll join them soon enough. But for tonight, on this episode of *Graveyard Paradise*, we say goodbye to those we've lost by visiting them where they are most comfortable: at home.

"We bid *adieu* to the romances by sleeping in the bedrooms of ex-lovers. We visit bygone friends by sipping tea in their living rooms. And we wait.

"We wait for them to stop by and say goodbye. Some of us will be waiting until we ourselves pass from this plane and become one with the grave. We think we know what horrors the sepulchres hold, but I am here to tell you: You have no idea."

Peter smiled into the camera, a slight grin that he learned from Connor. He raised his hand and pointed at the mausoleum in the background. The spotlight flashed bright white to reveal the names on two headstones in the makeshift graveyard: one for Diana and one for Connor.

"You have no idea what can cry down the dark," Peter said.

THE END

About the Author

T.J. Tranchell was raised in Utah and lives in Moscow, Idaho, with his wife, Savannah, and their son, Clark. He holds a Master's degree in literature from Central Washington University. His short stories have appeared in *Despumation Vol. 1*, "Mad Scientist Journal," and *GIVE: An Anthology of Anatomical Entries*, which he co-edited with author Michelle Kilmer.

Tranchell has been a journalist, a grocery store janitor, a customer service clerk, and occasional fast food employee. He has found his place in writing fiction and teaching English and journalism.

Cry Down Dark is his first novel.

Author photo by Melissa Hartley

CPSIA information can be obtained
at www.ICGtesting.com
Printed in the USA
LVHW082332261020
669909LV00016B/1973

9 781940 247243